SIGN OFF

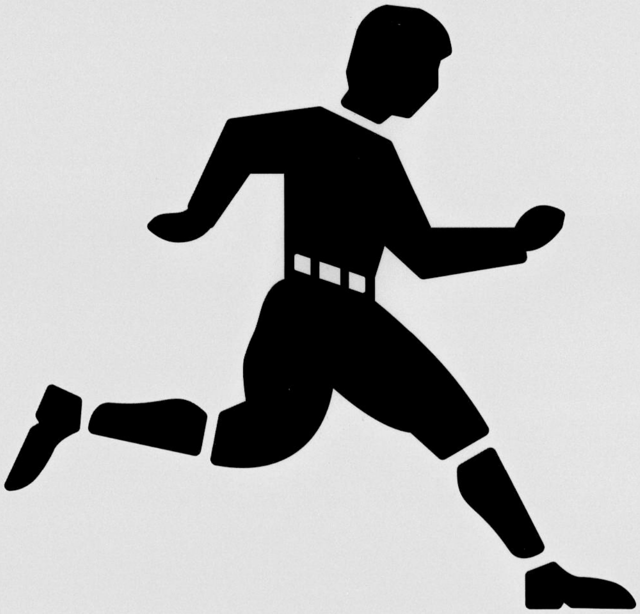

STEPHEN SAVAGE

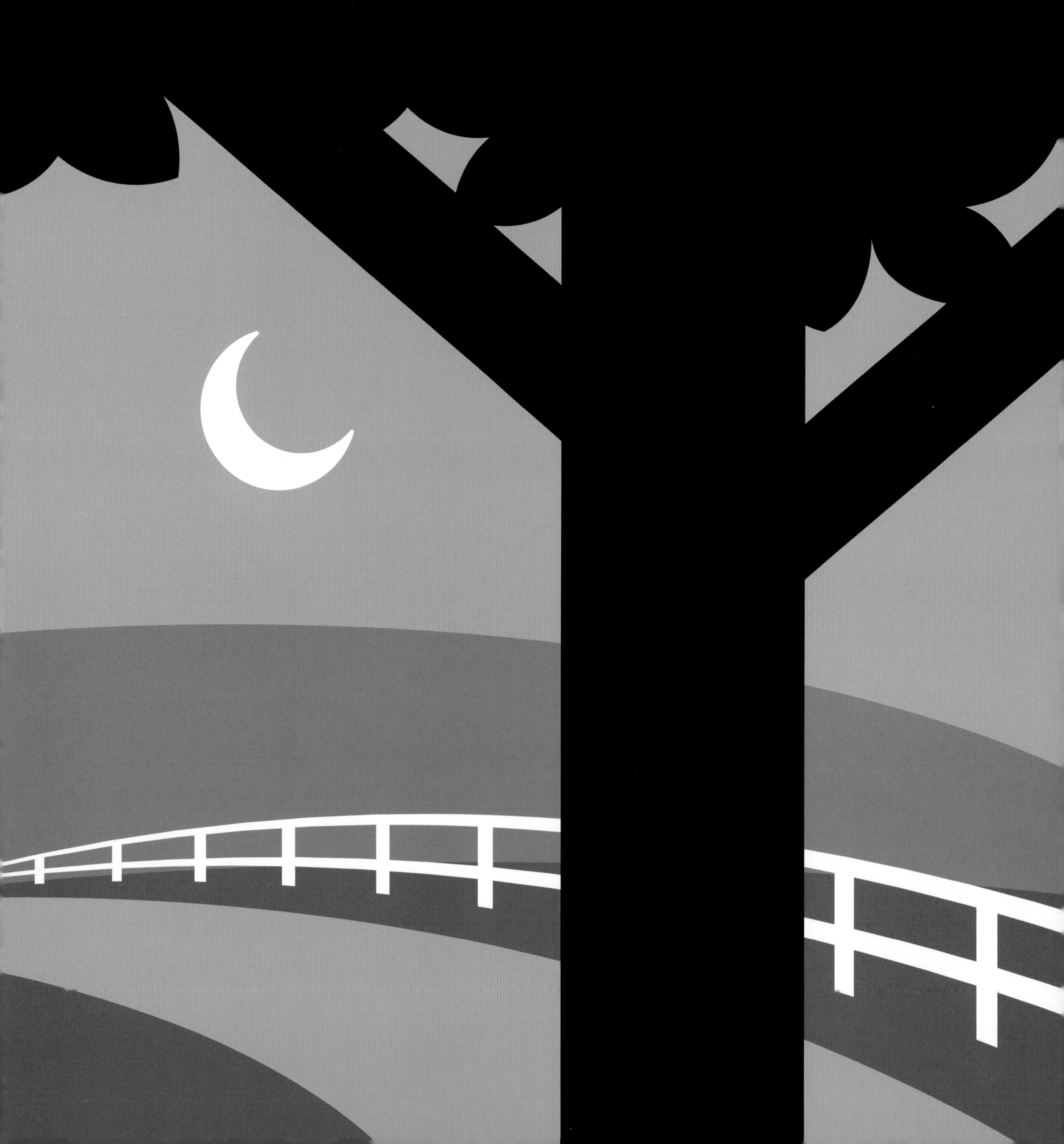

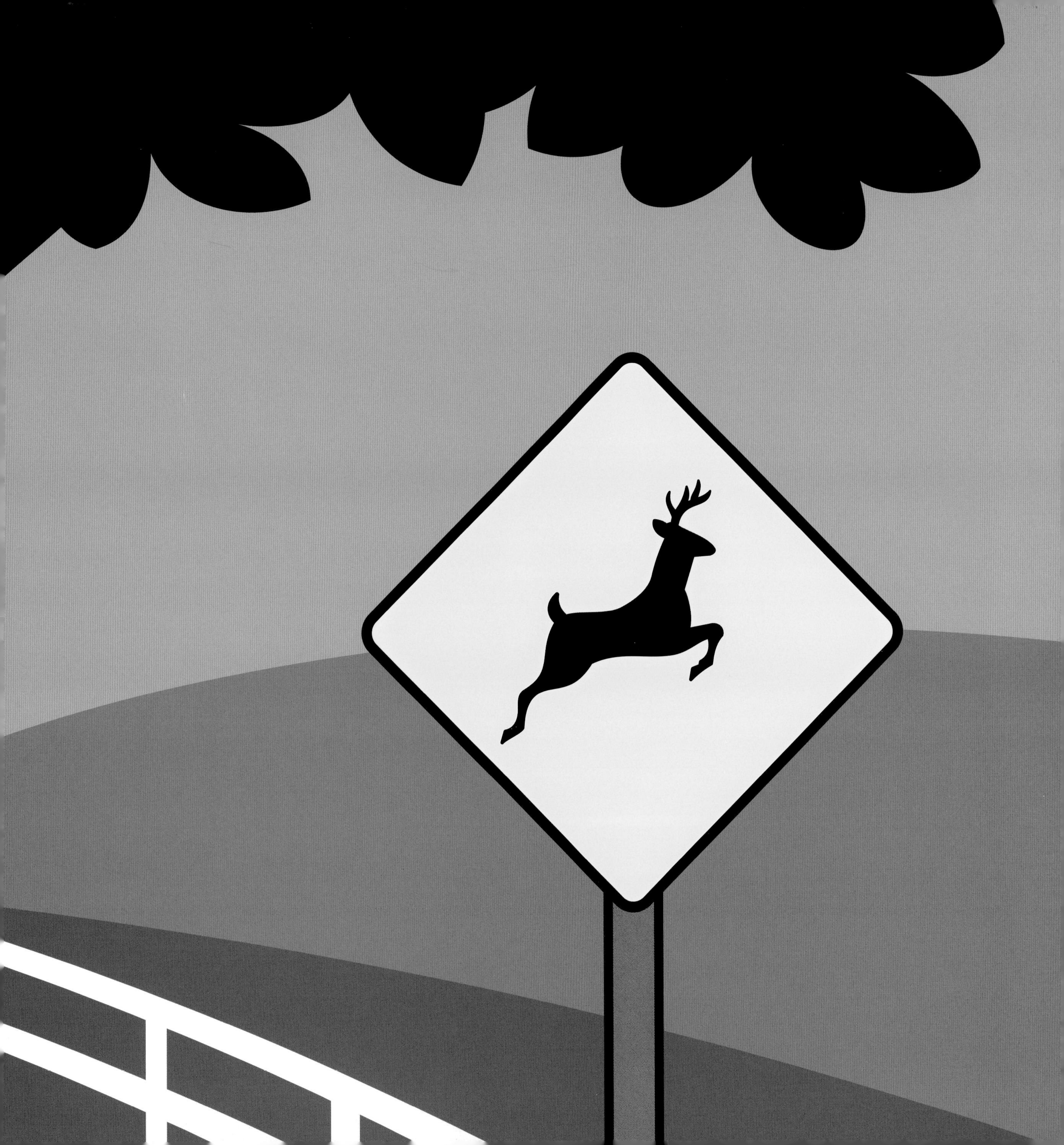

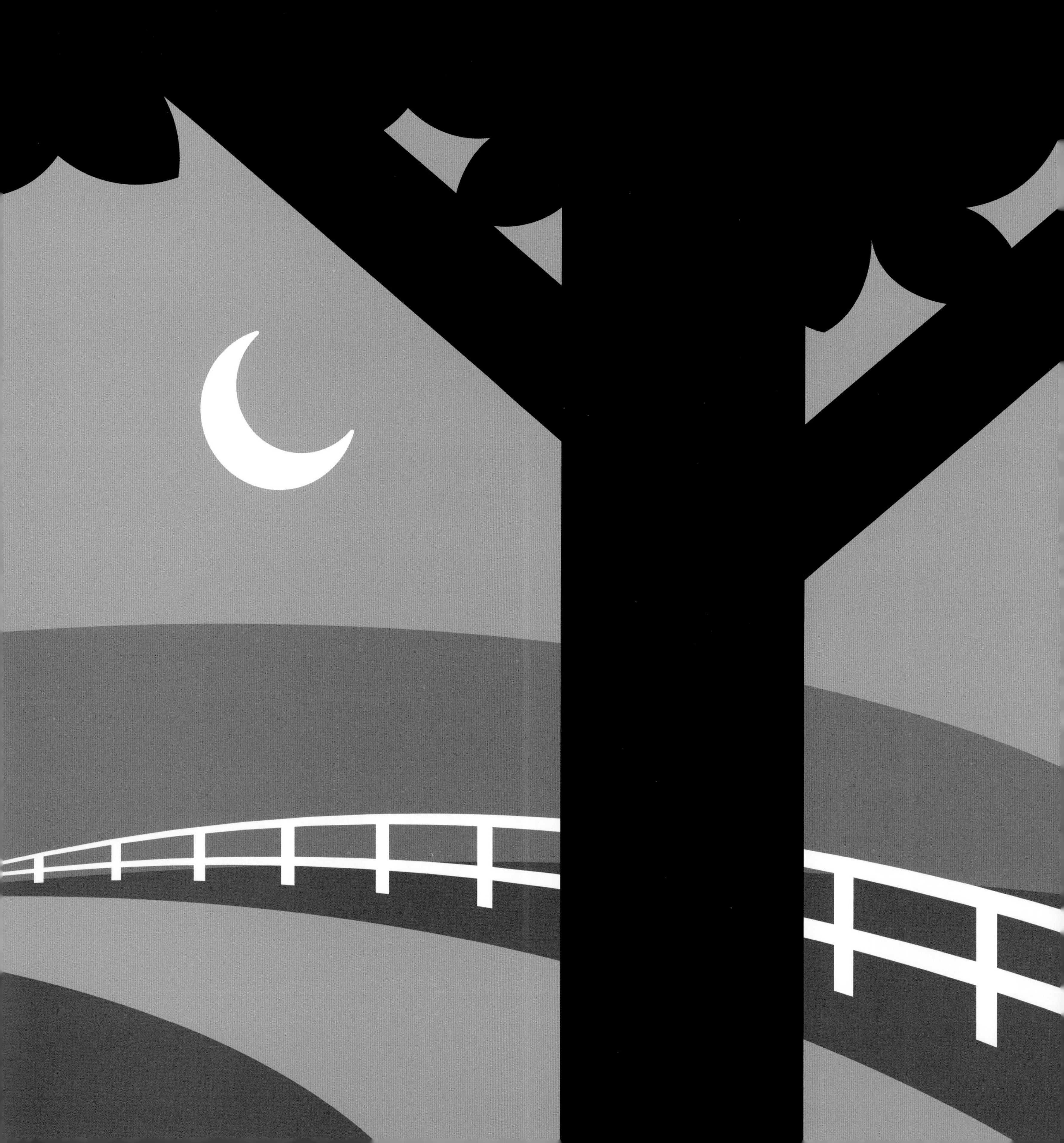

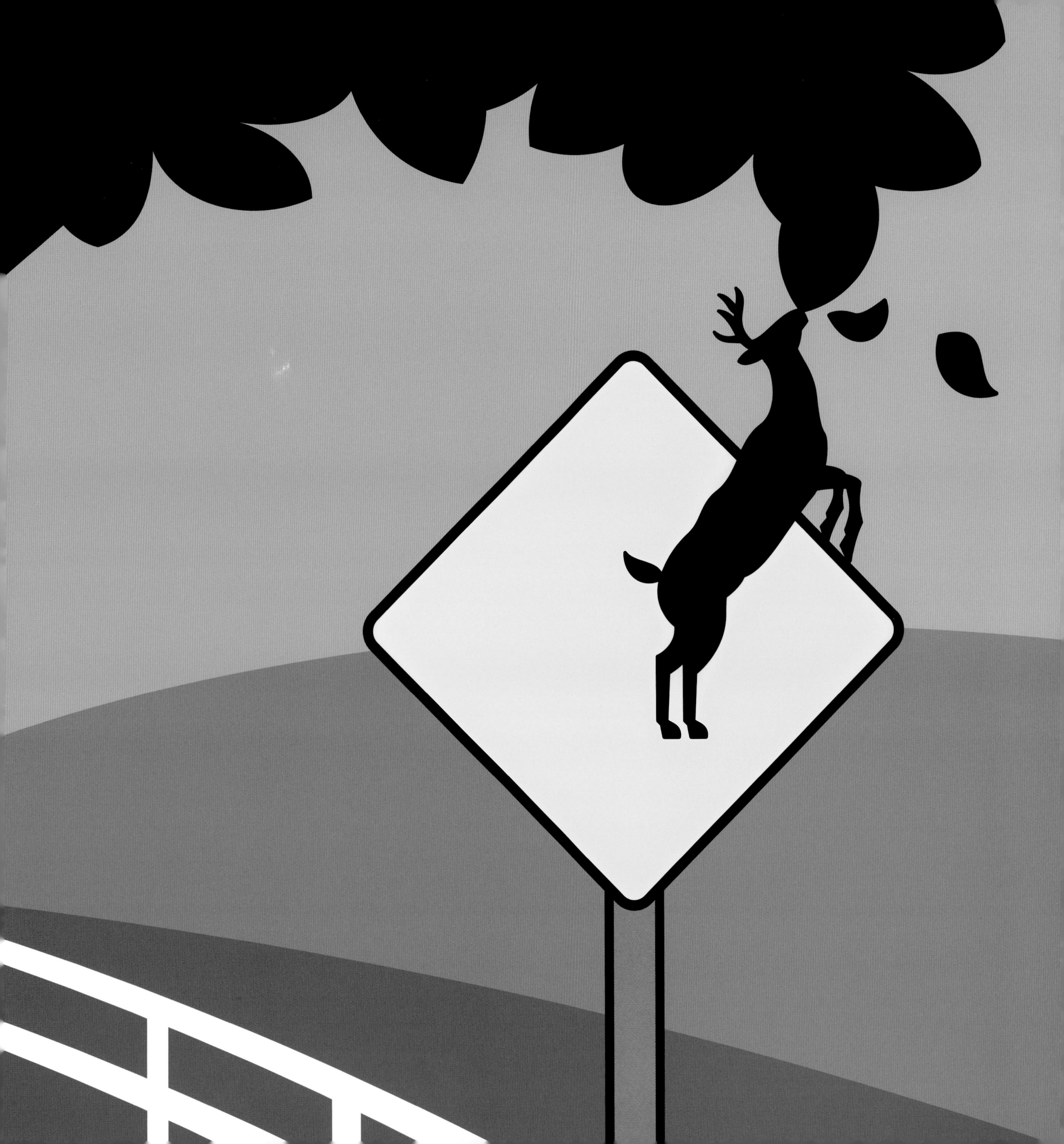

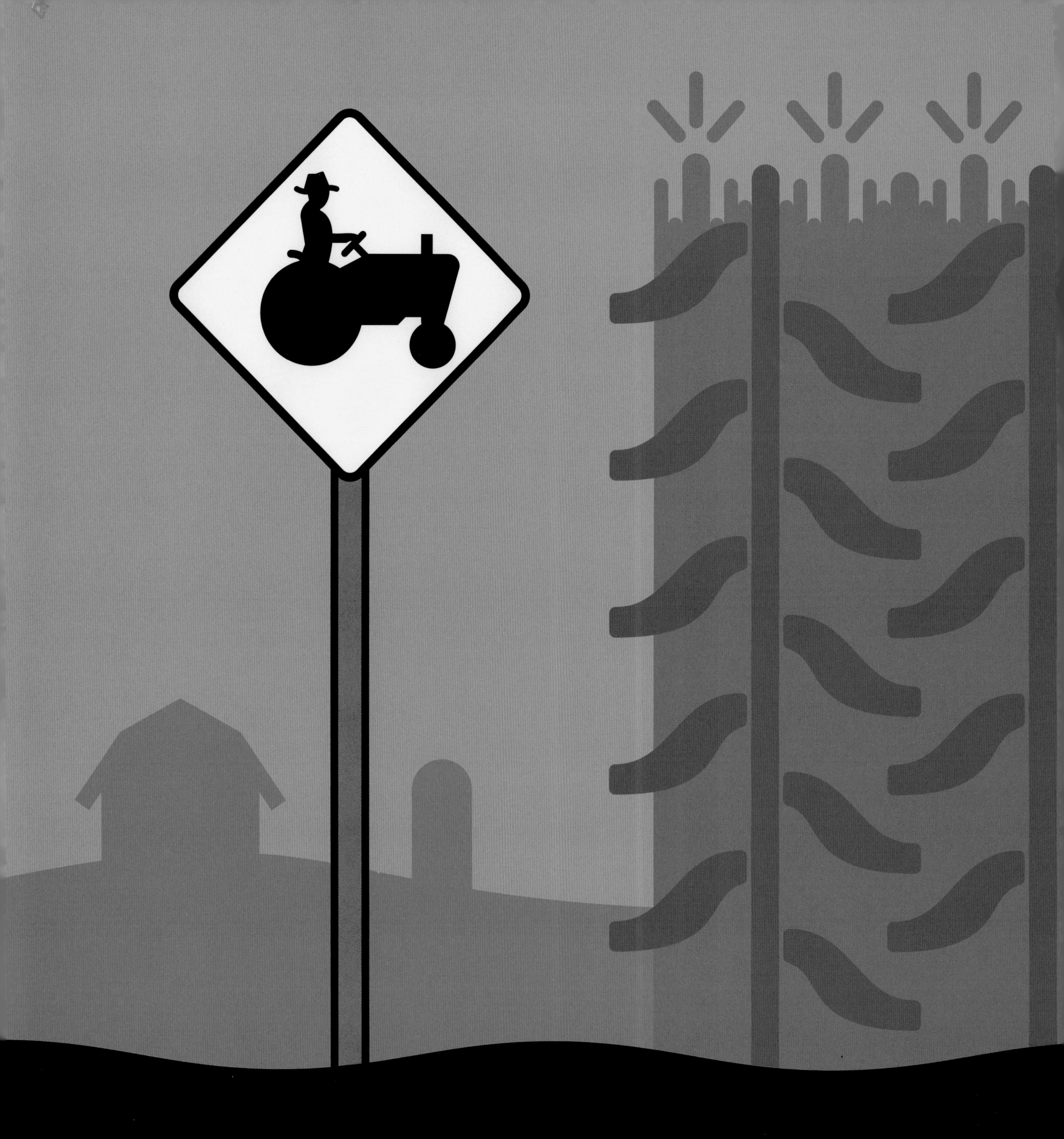

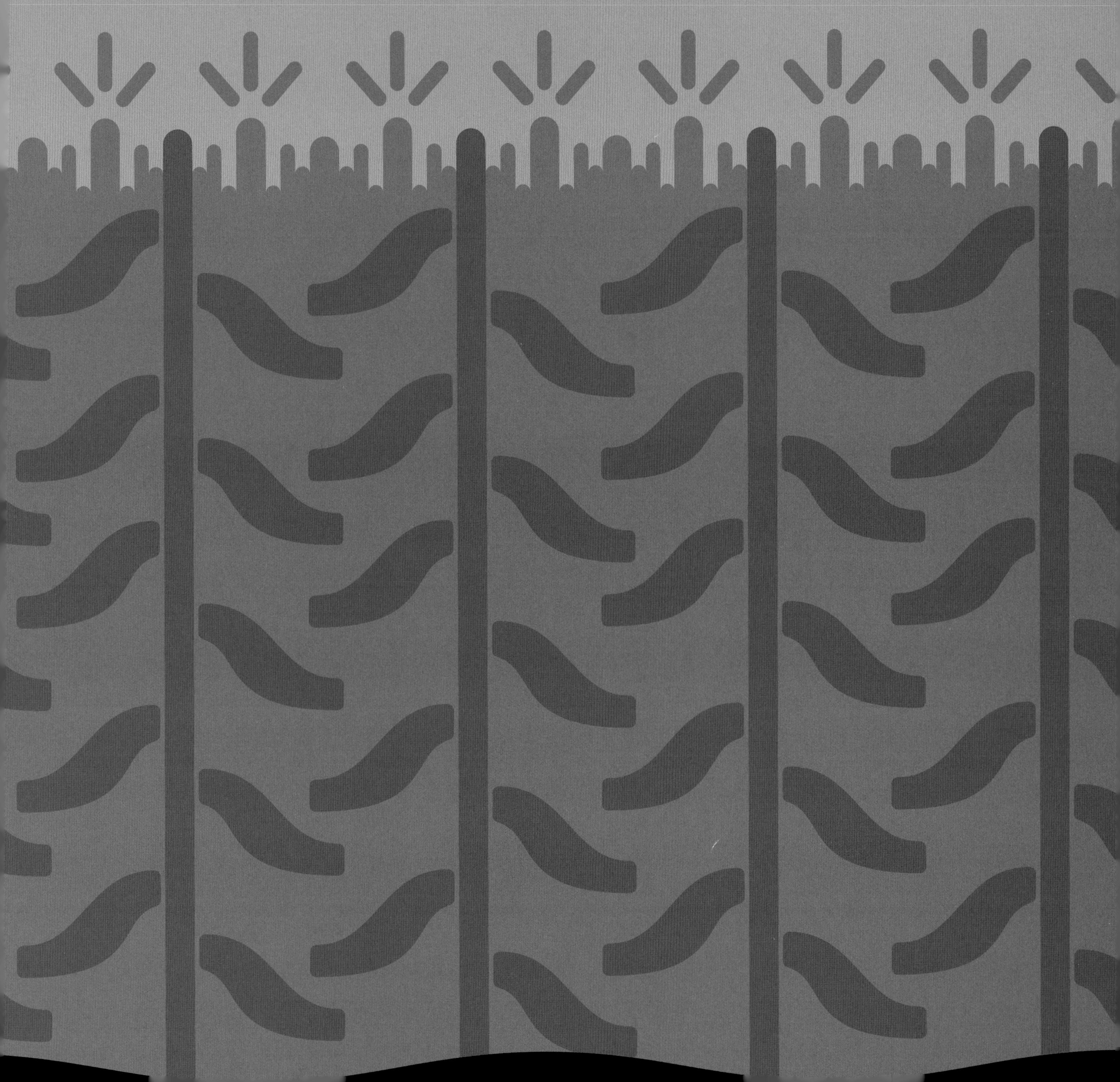

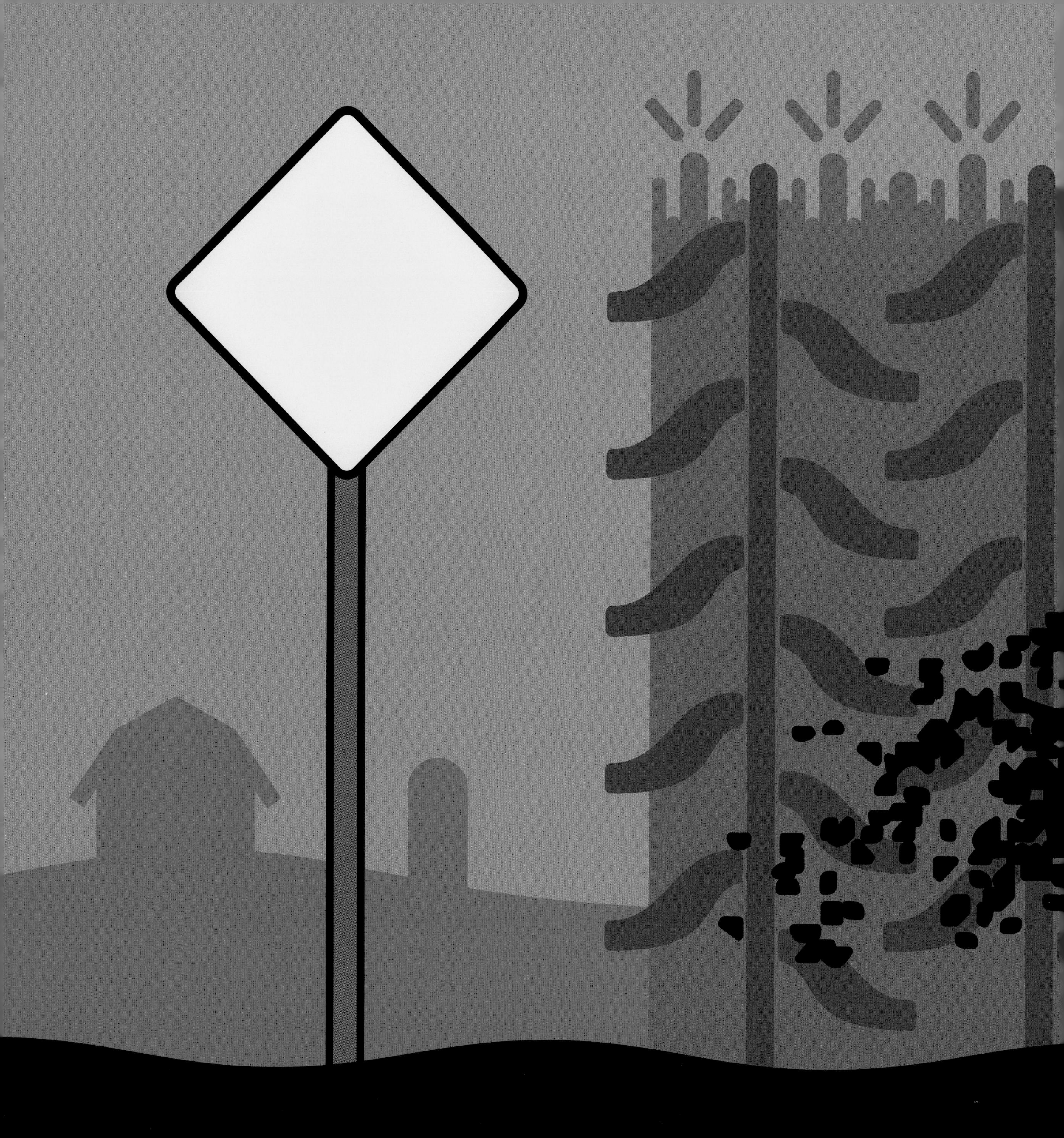

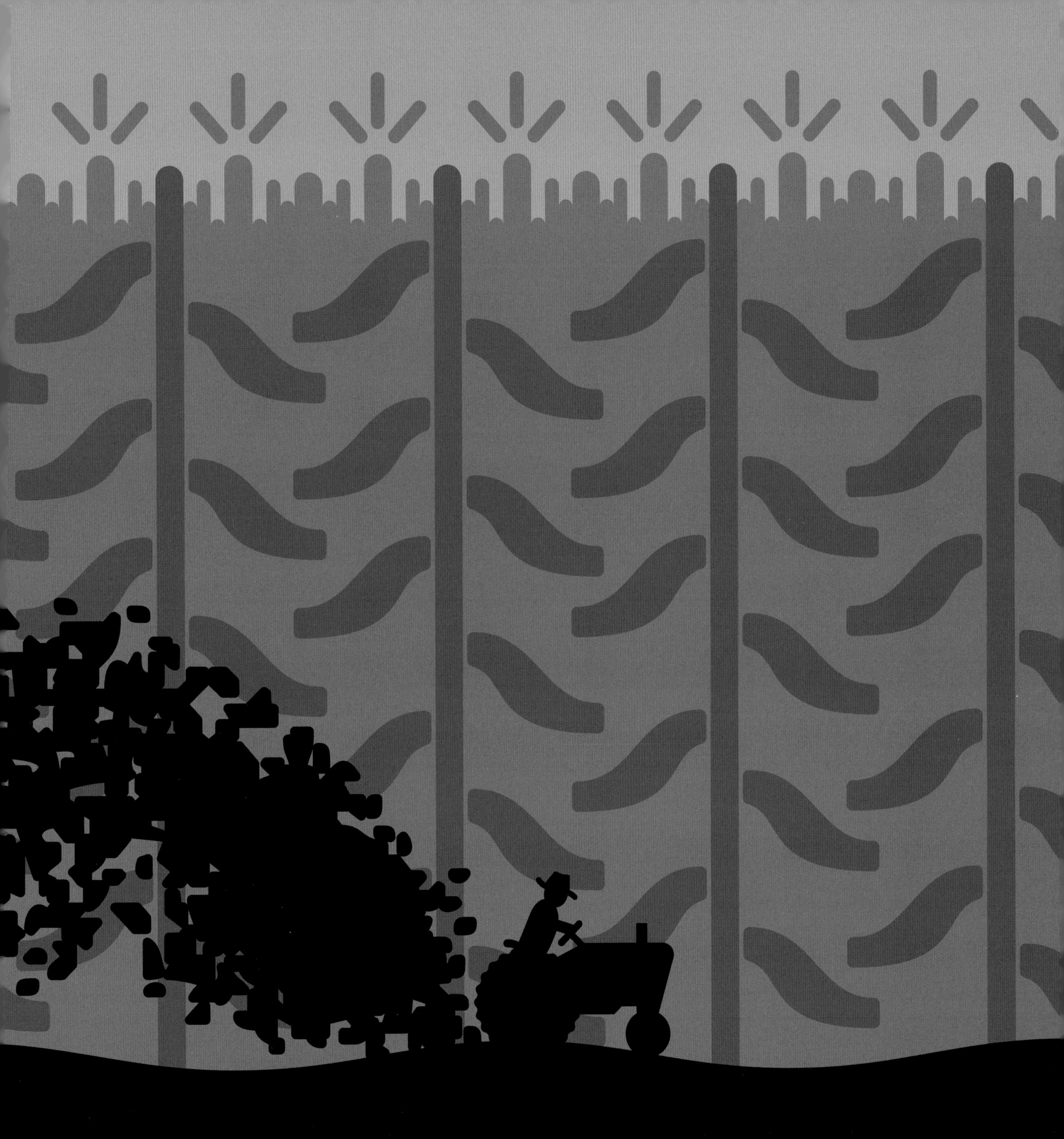

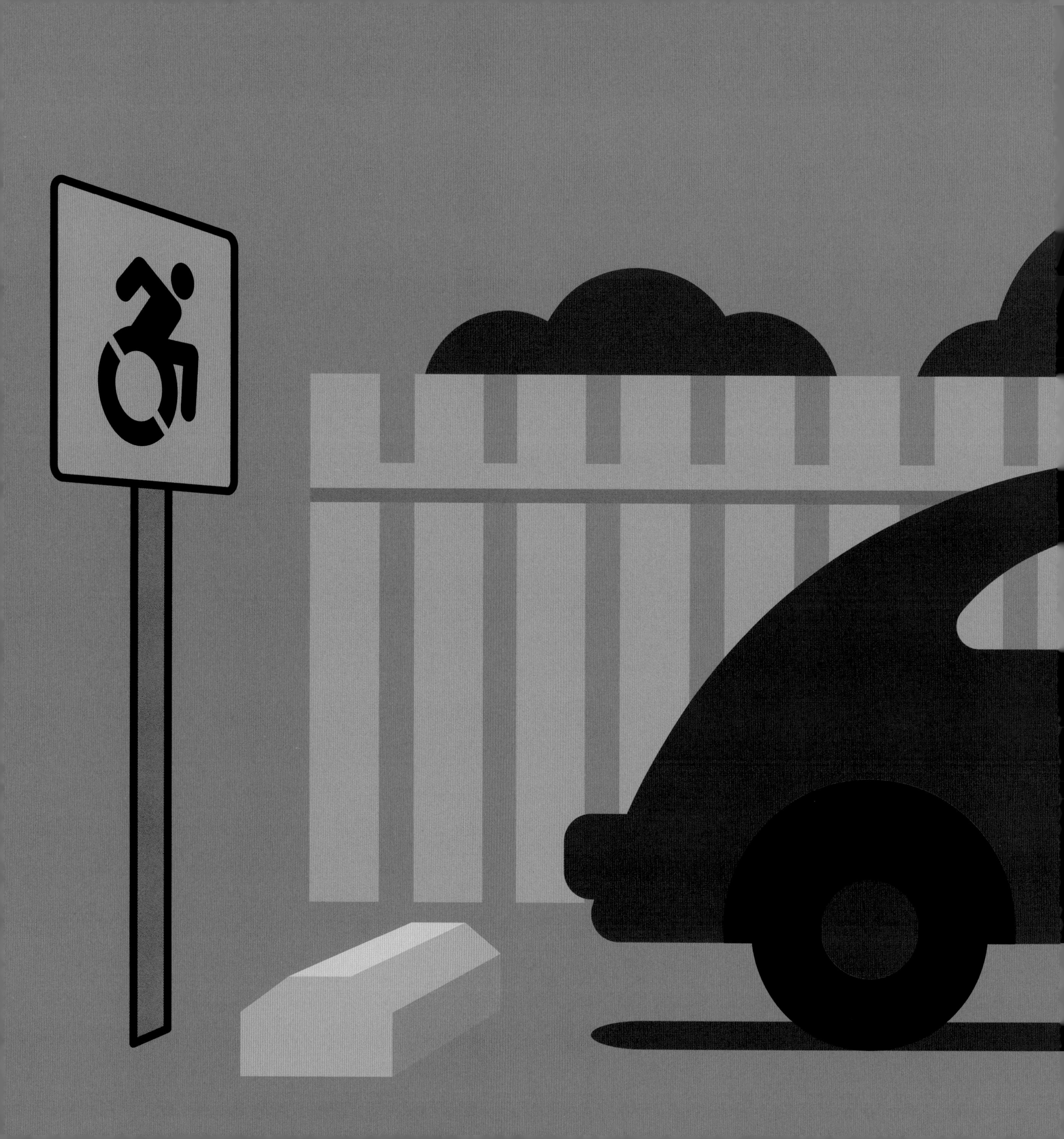

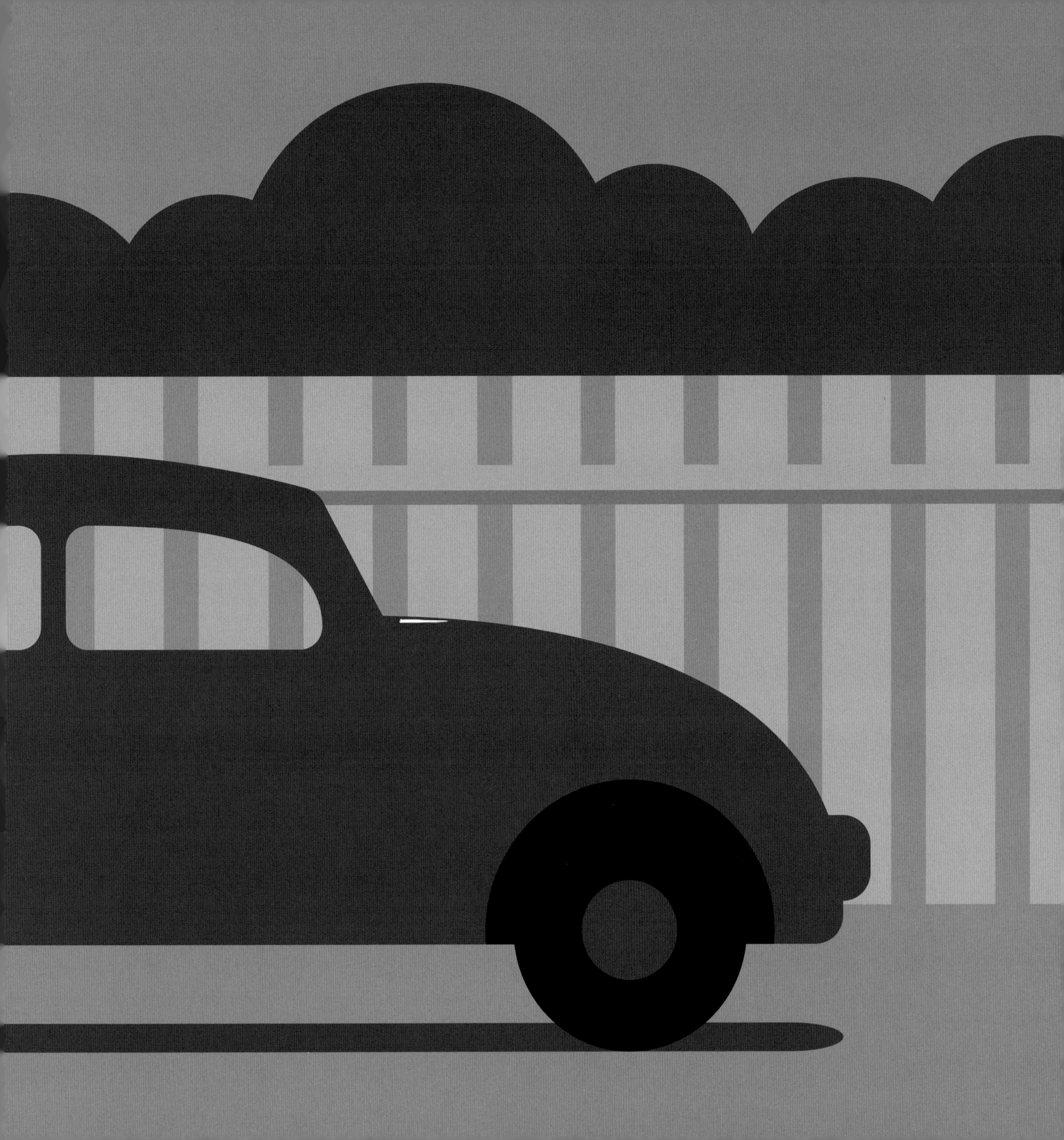

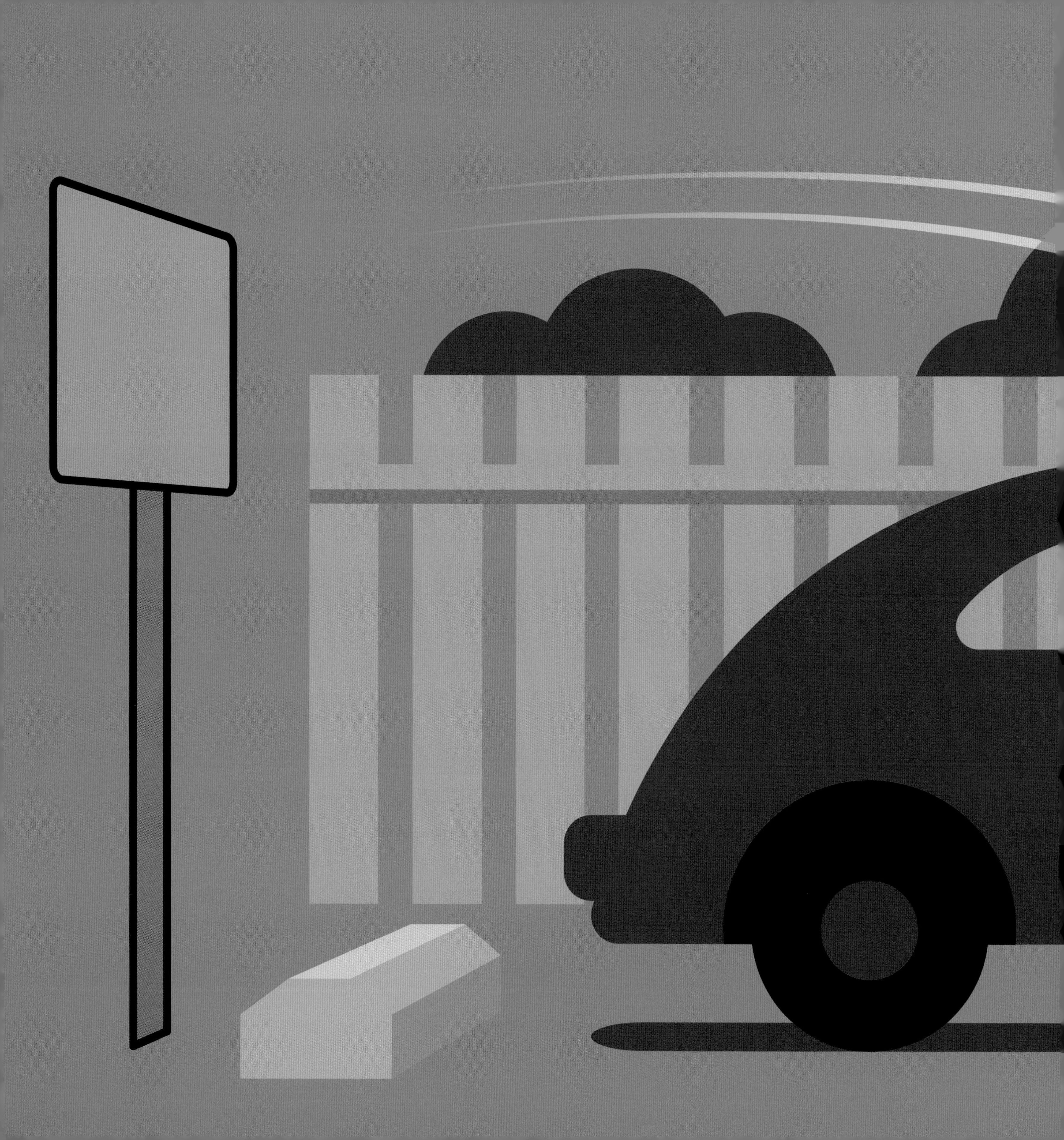

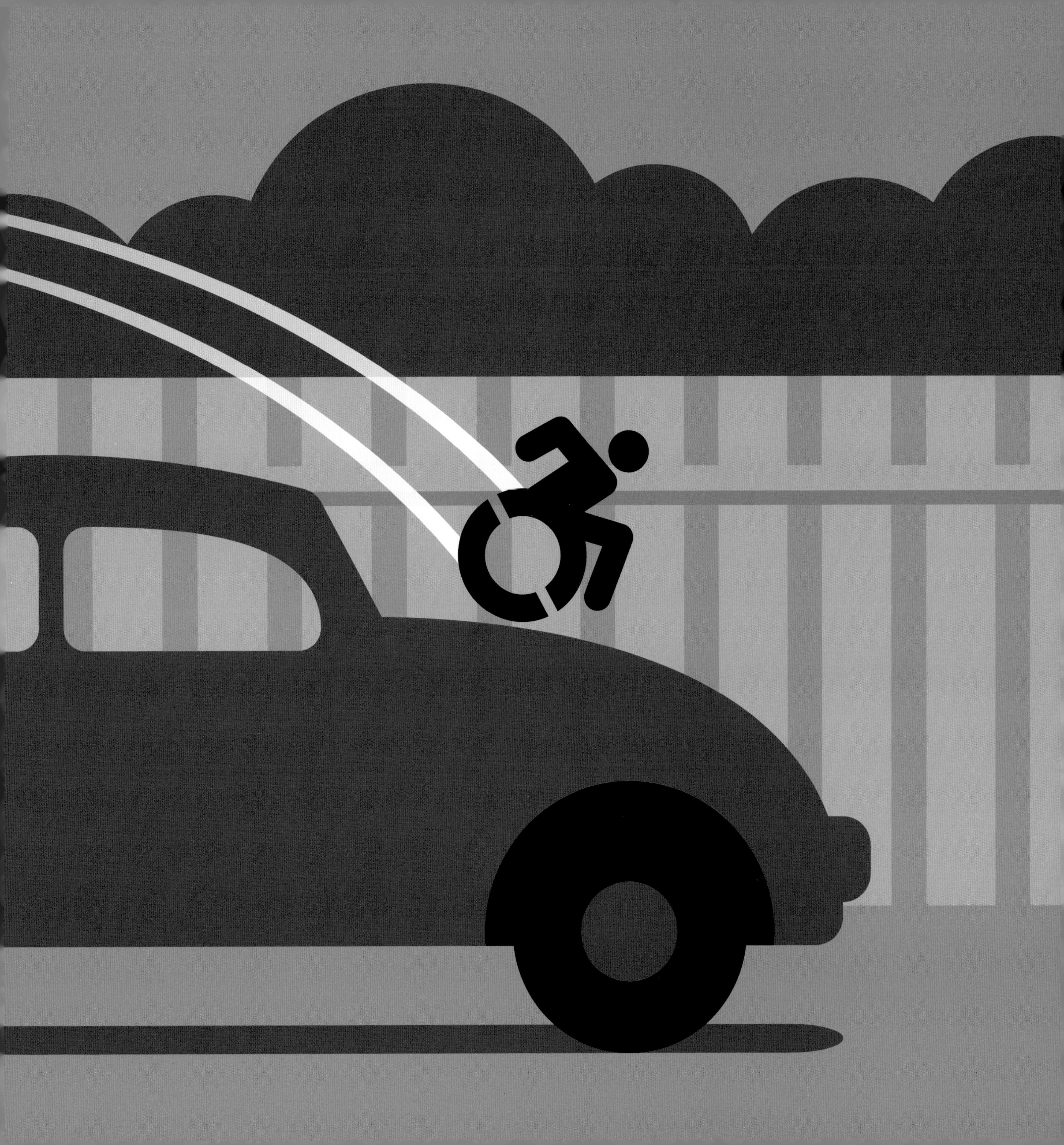

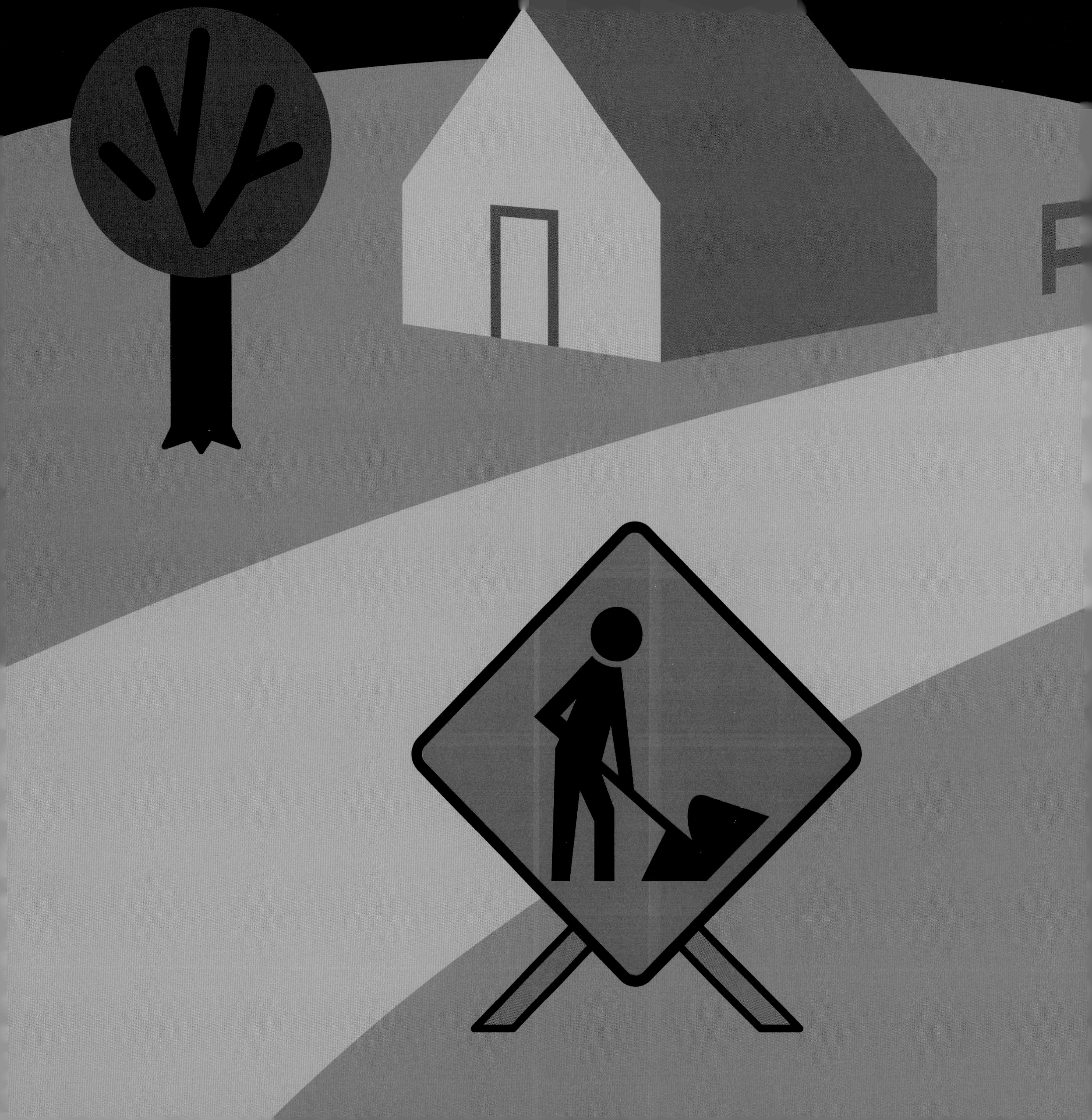

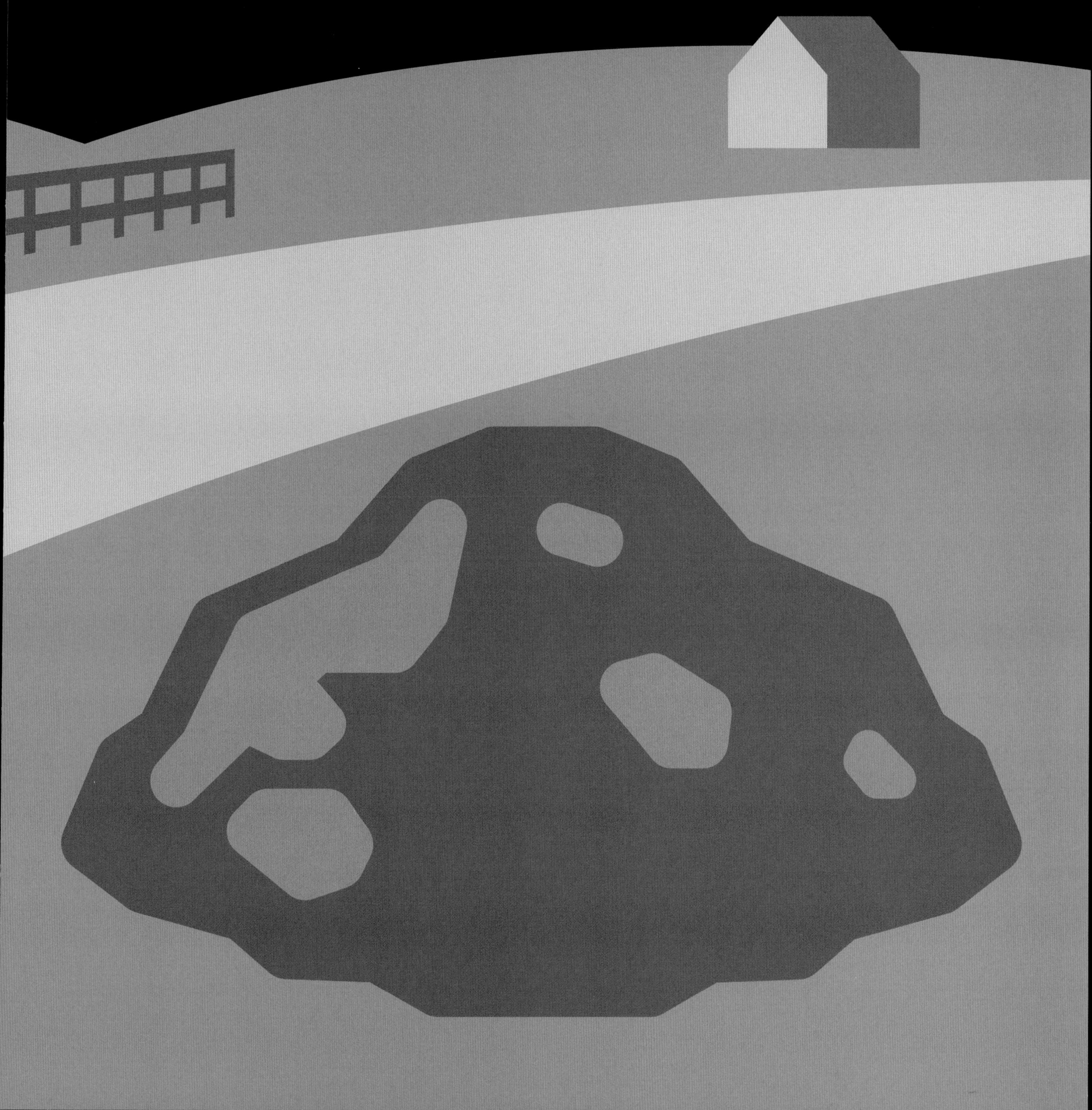

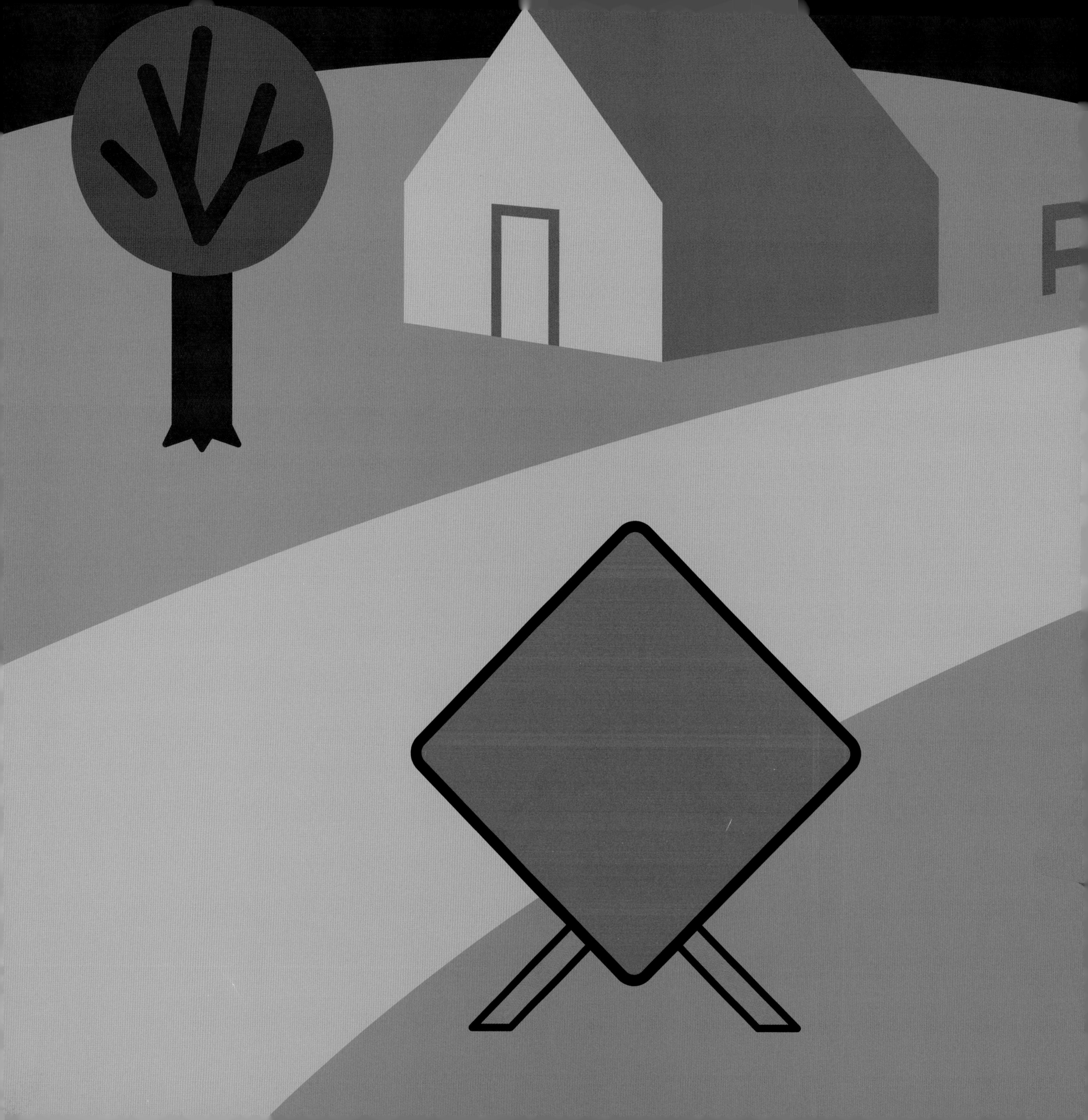

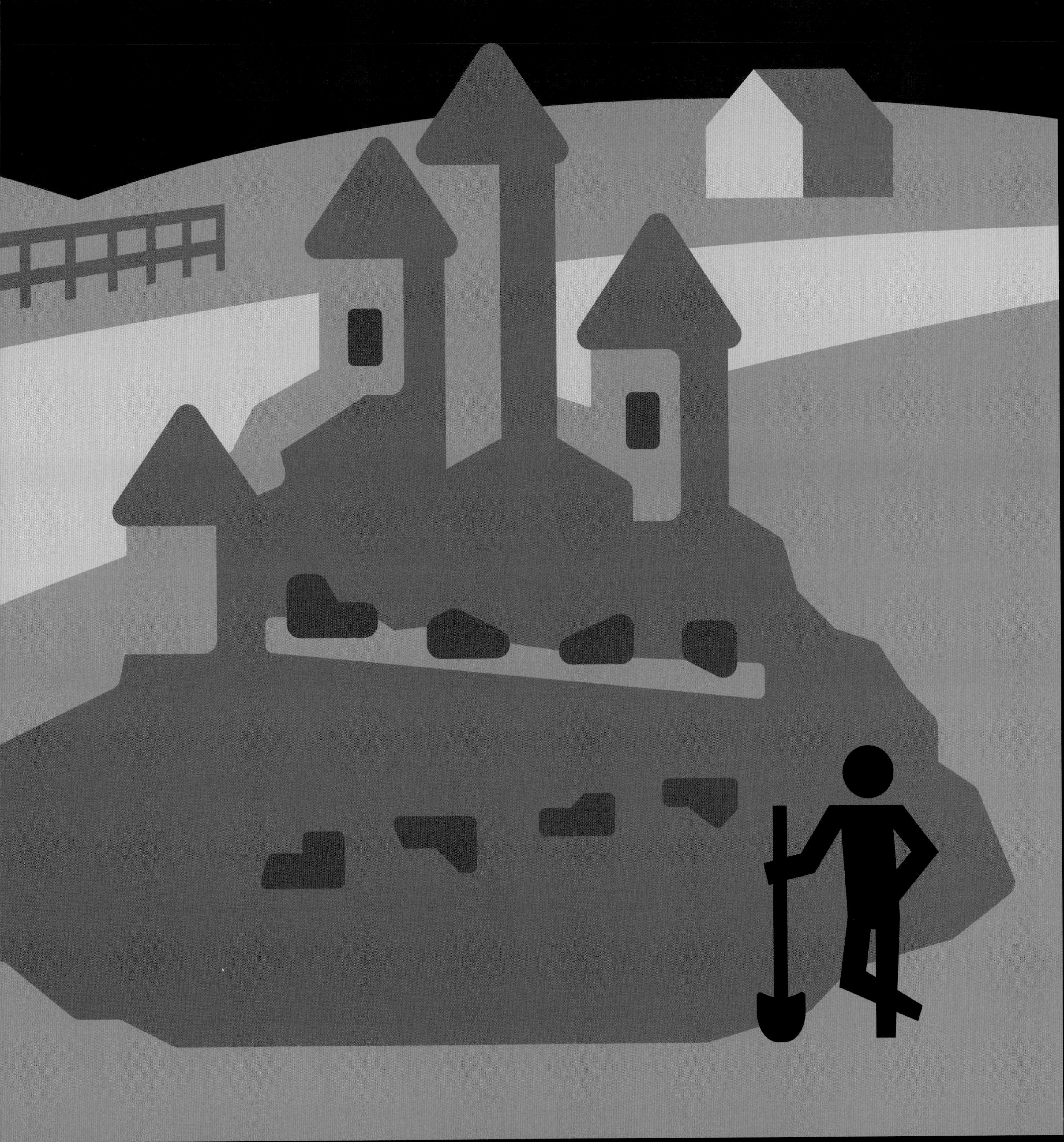

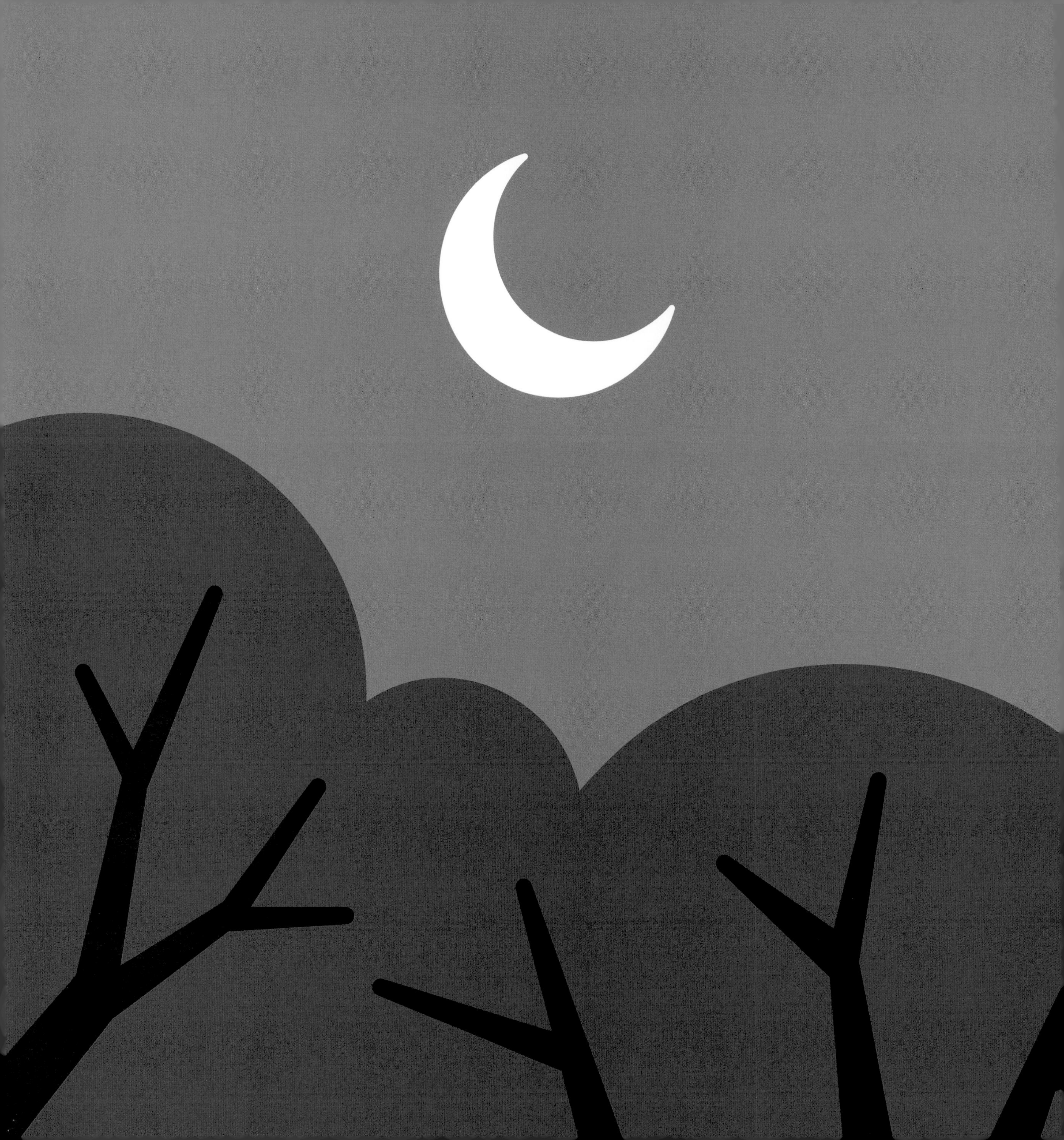

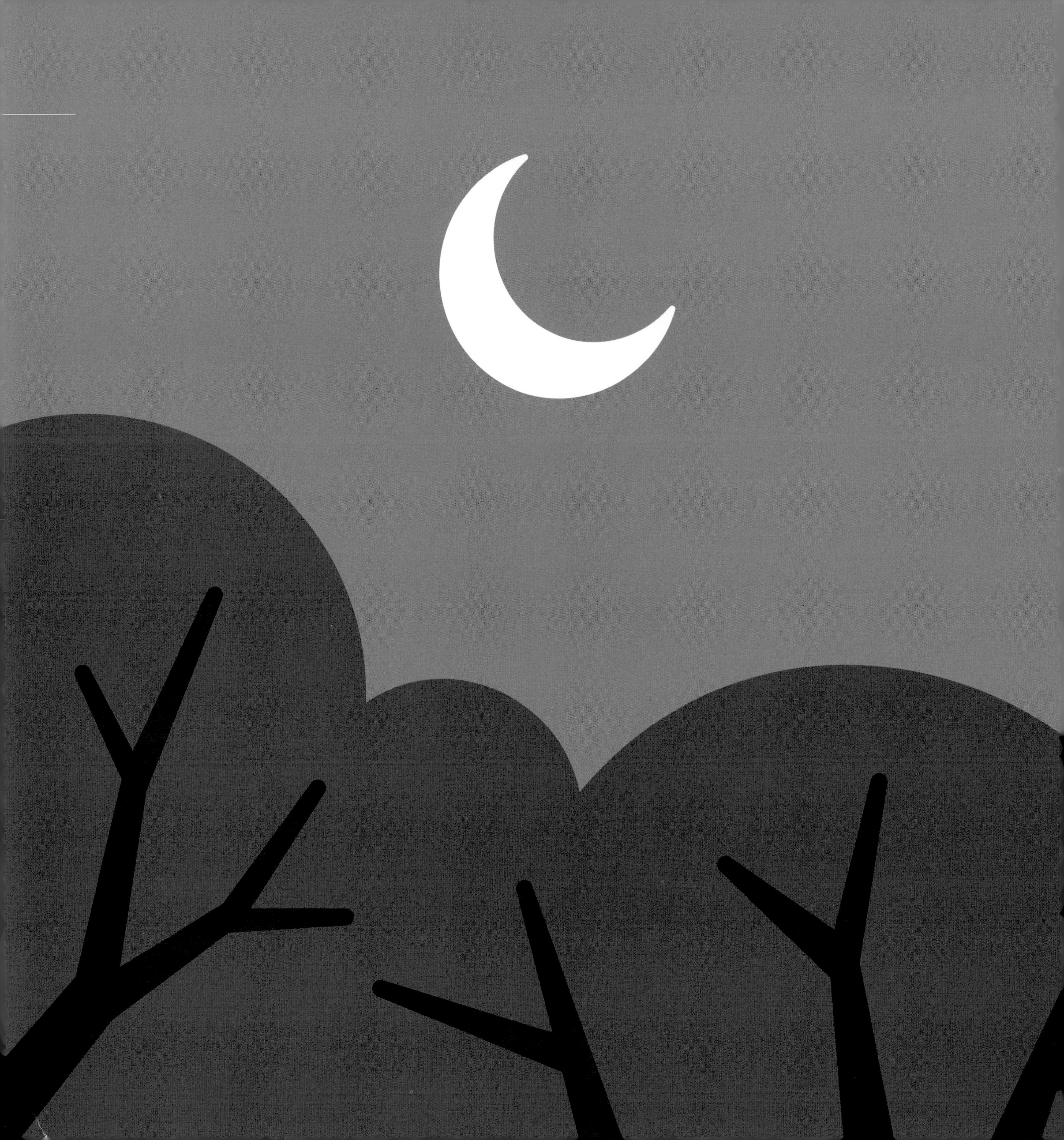

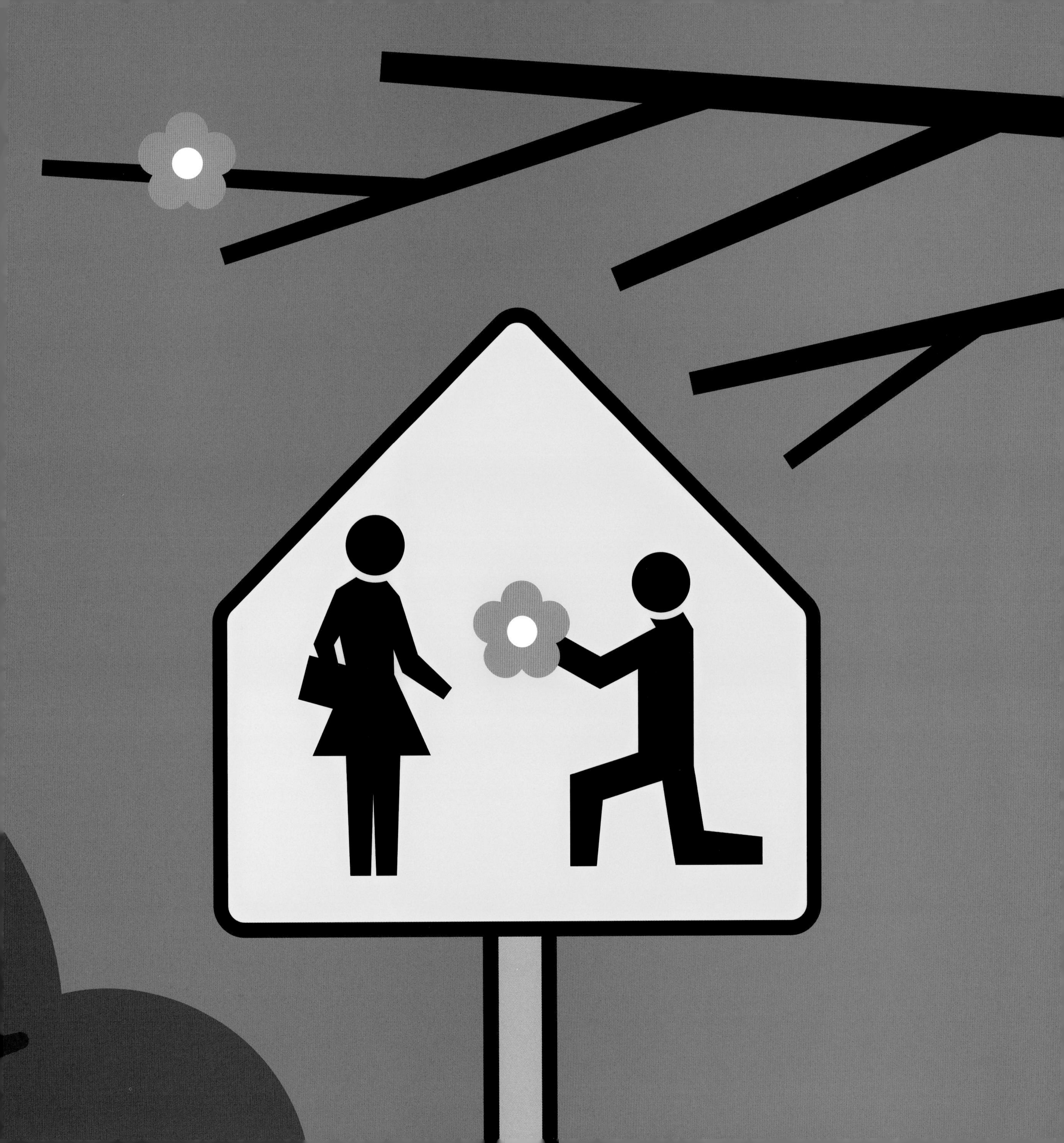

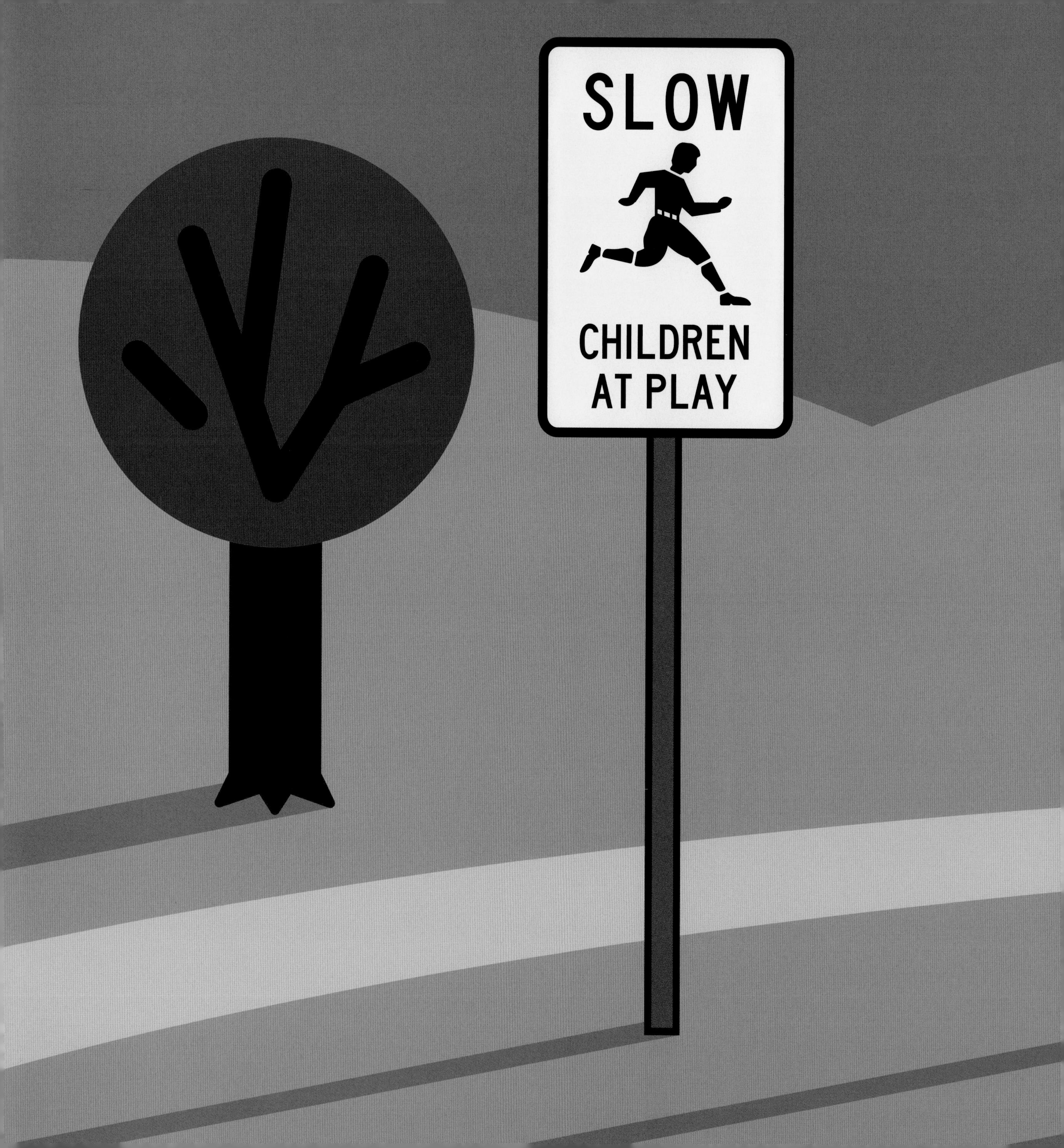
SLOW
CHILDREN
AT PLAY

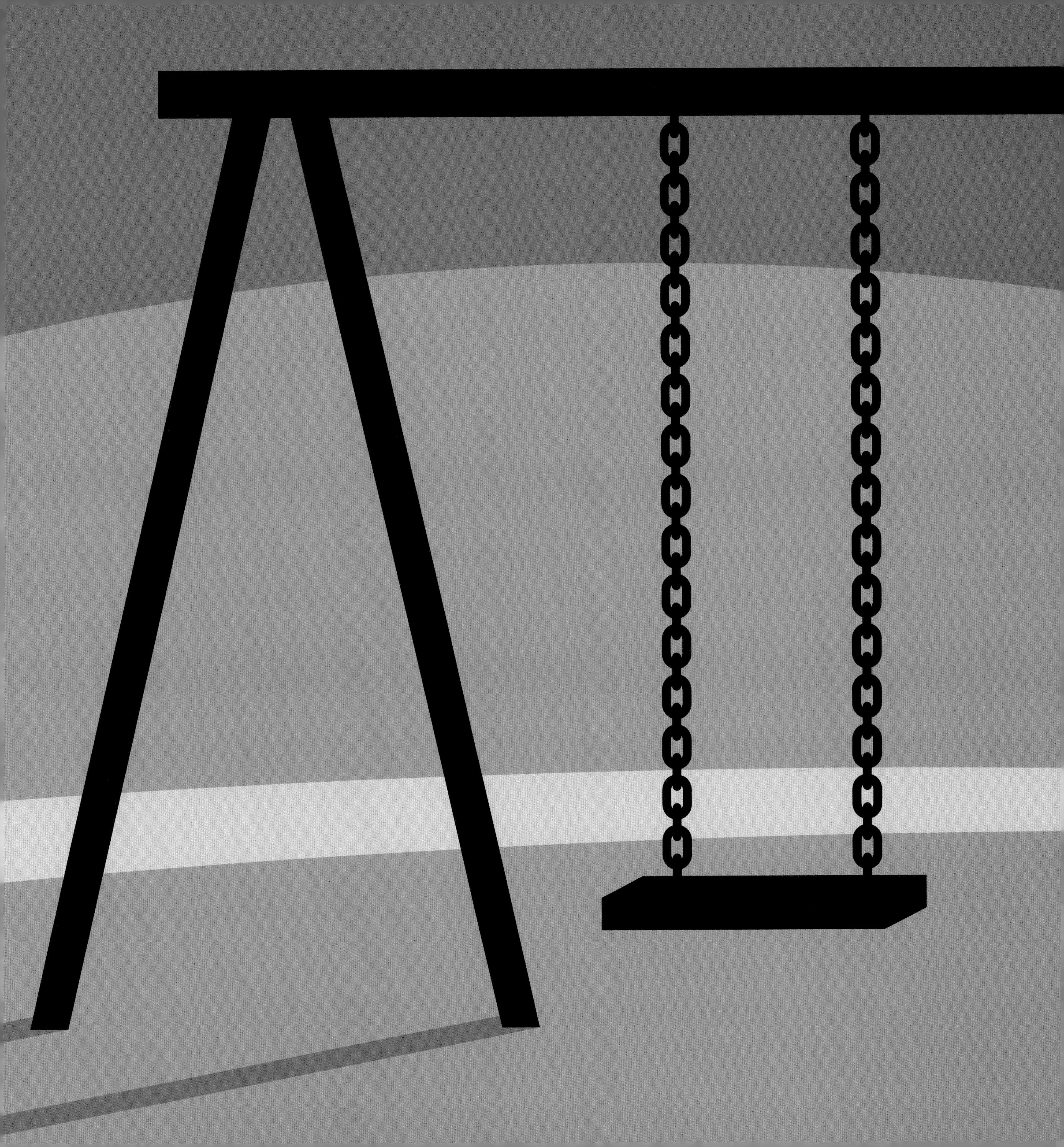

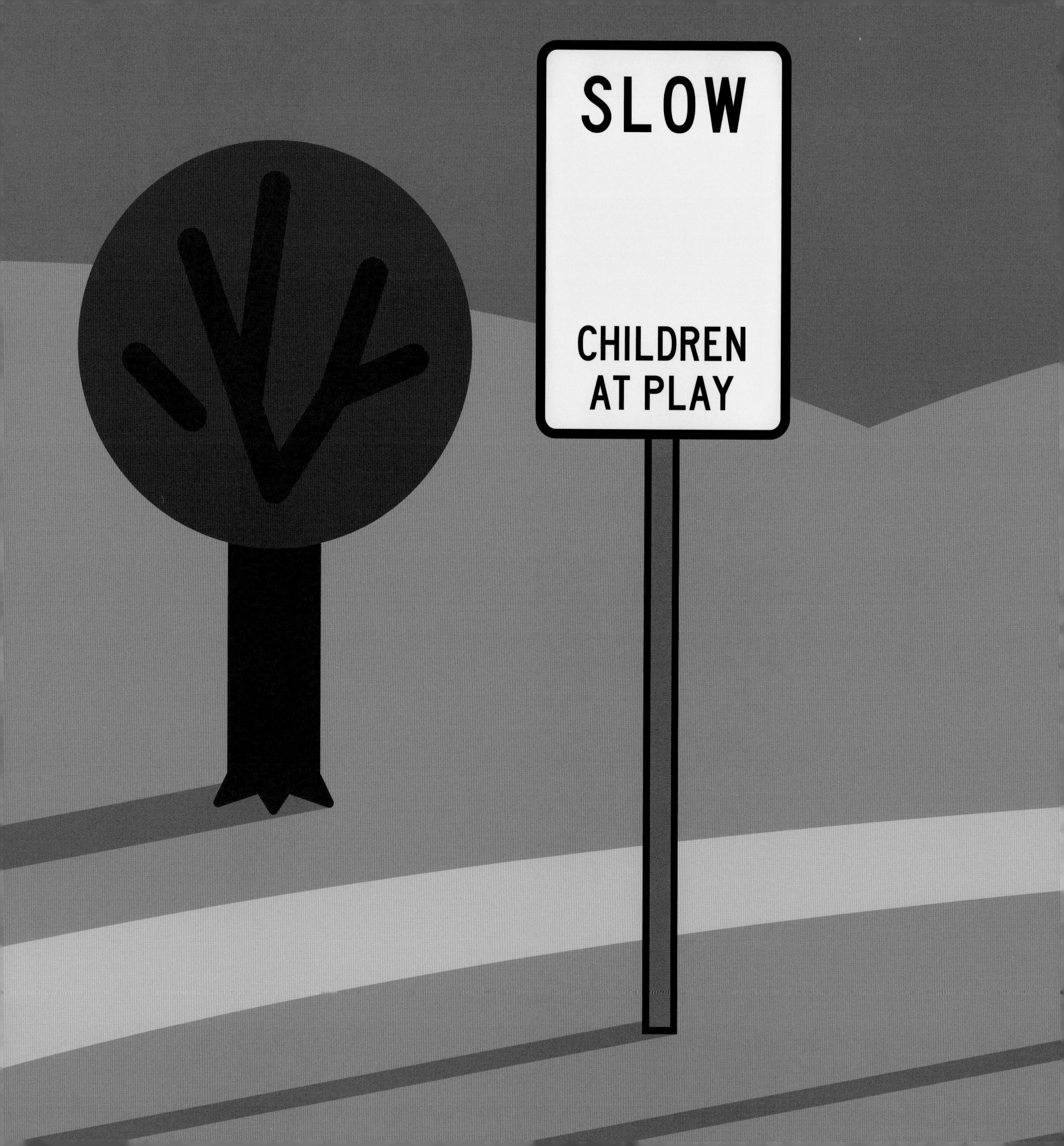
SLOW
CHILDREN
AT PLAY

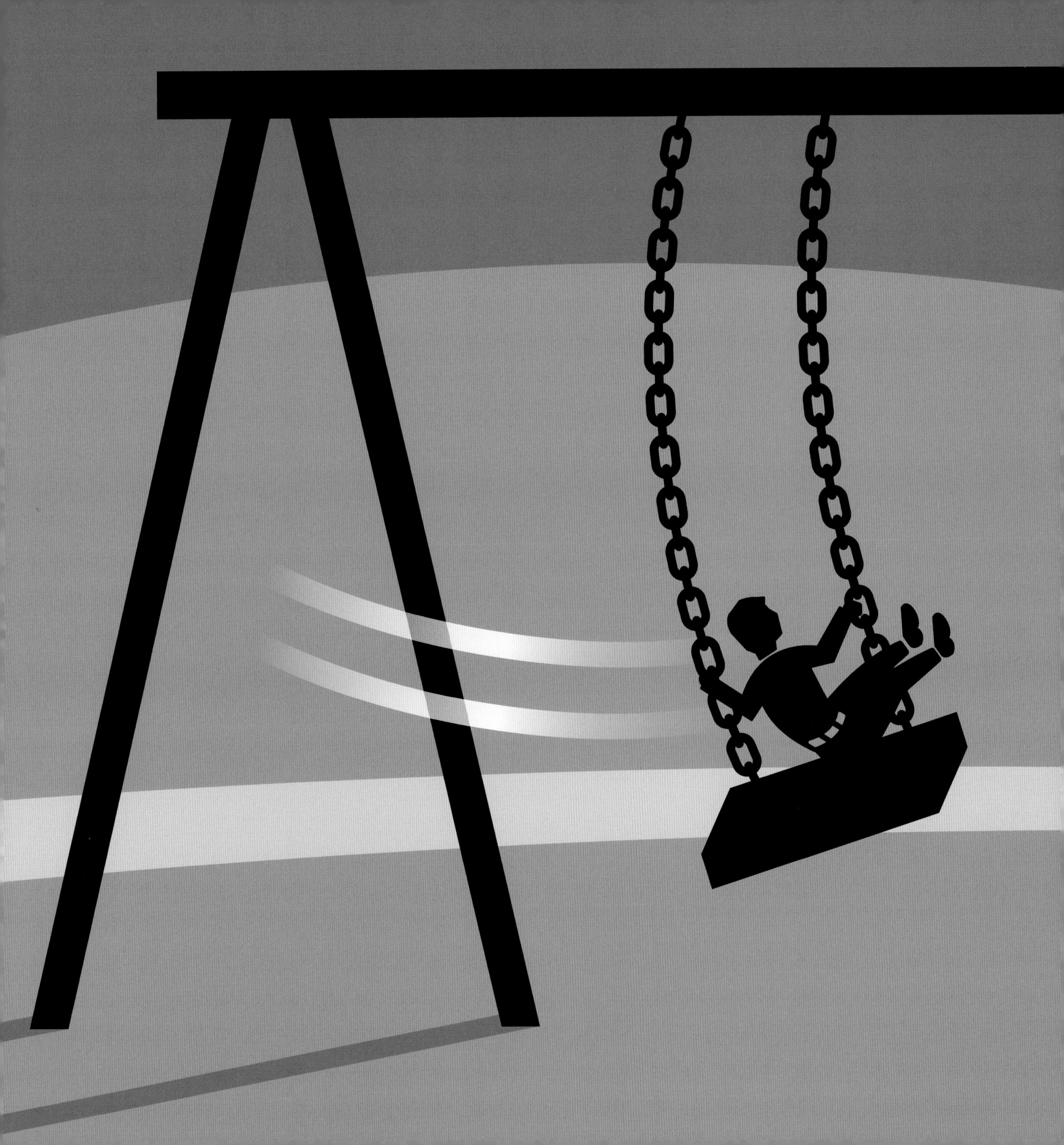

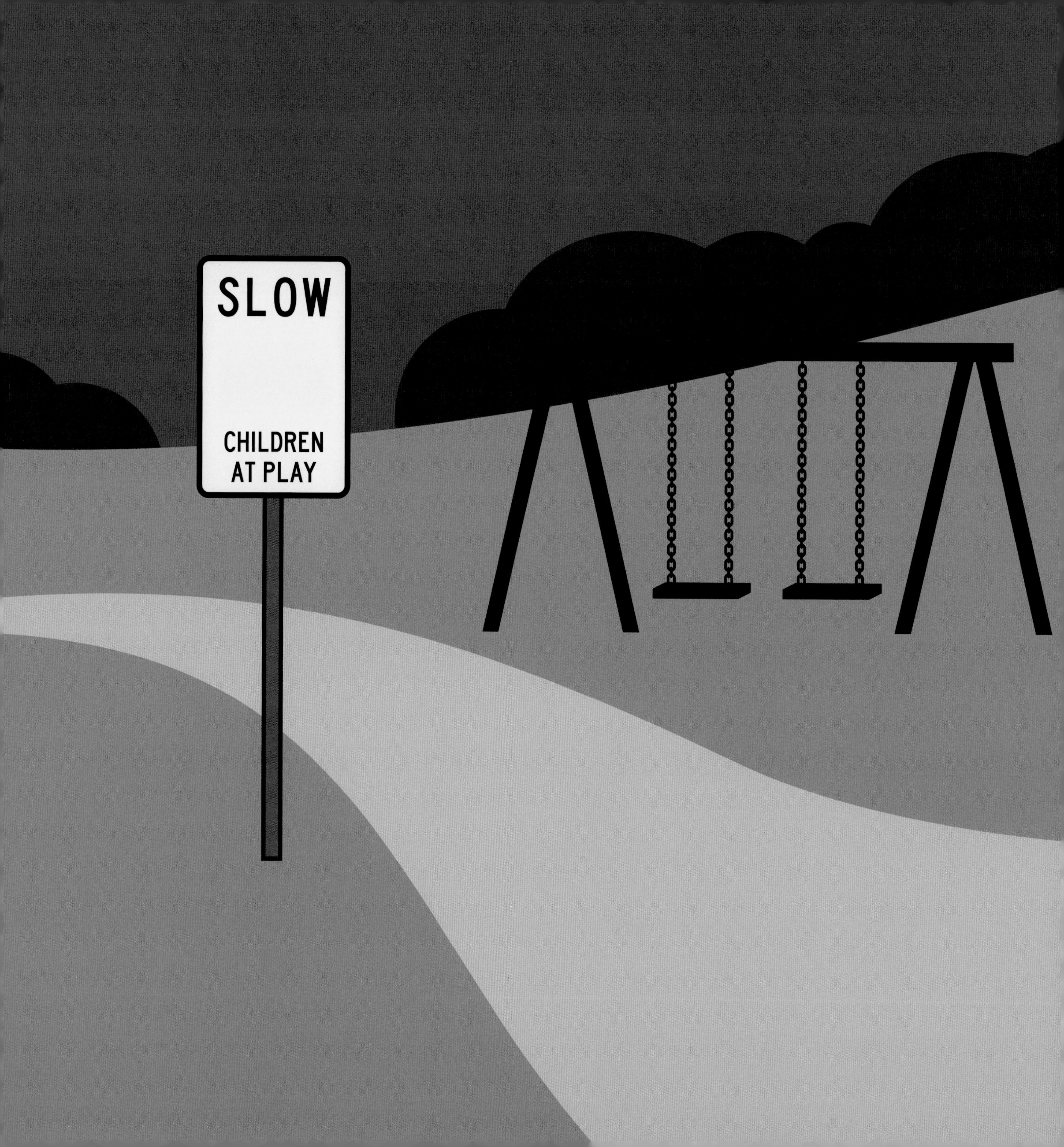
SLOW
CHILDREN
AT PLAY

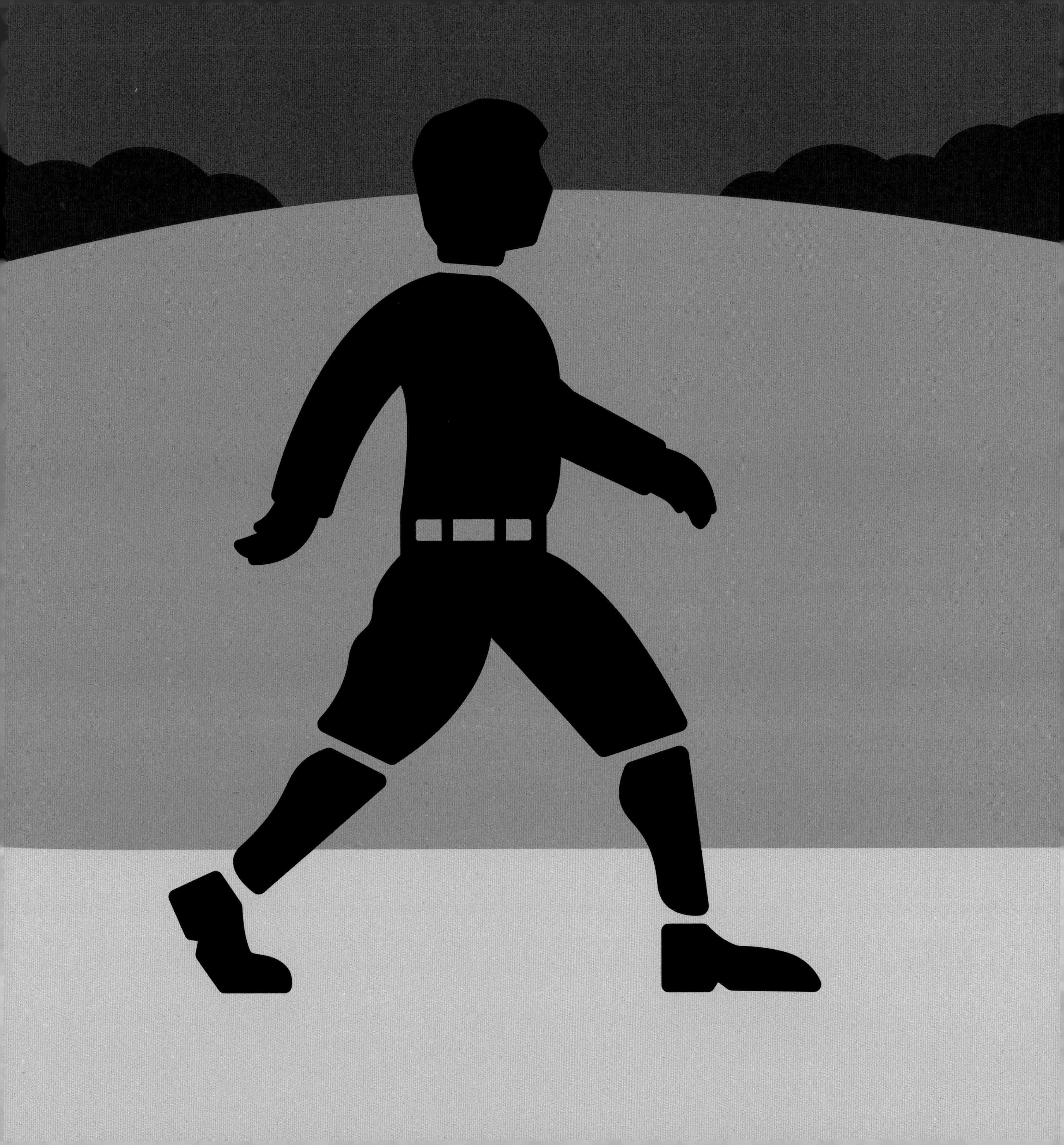

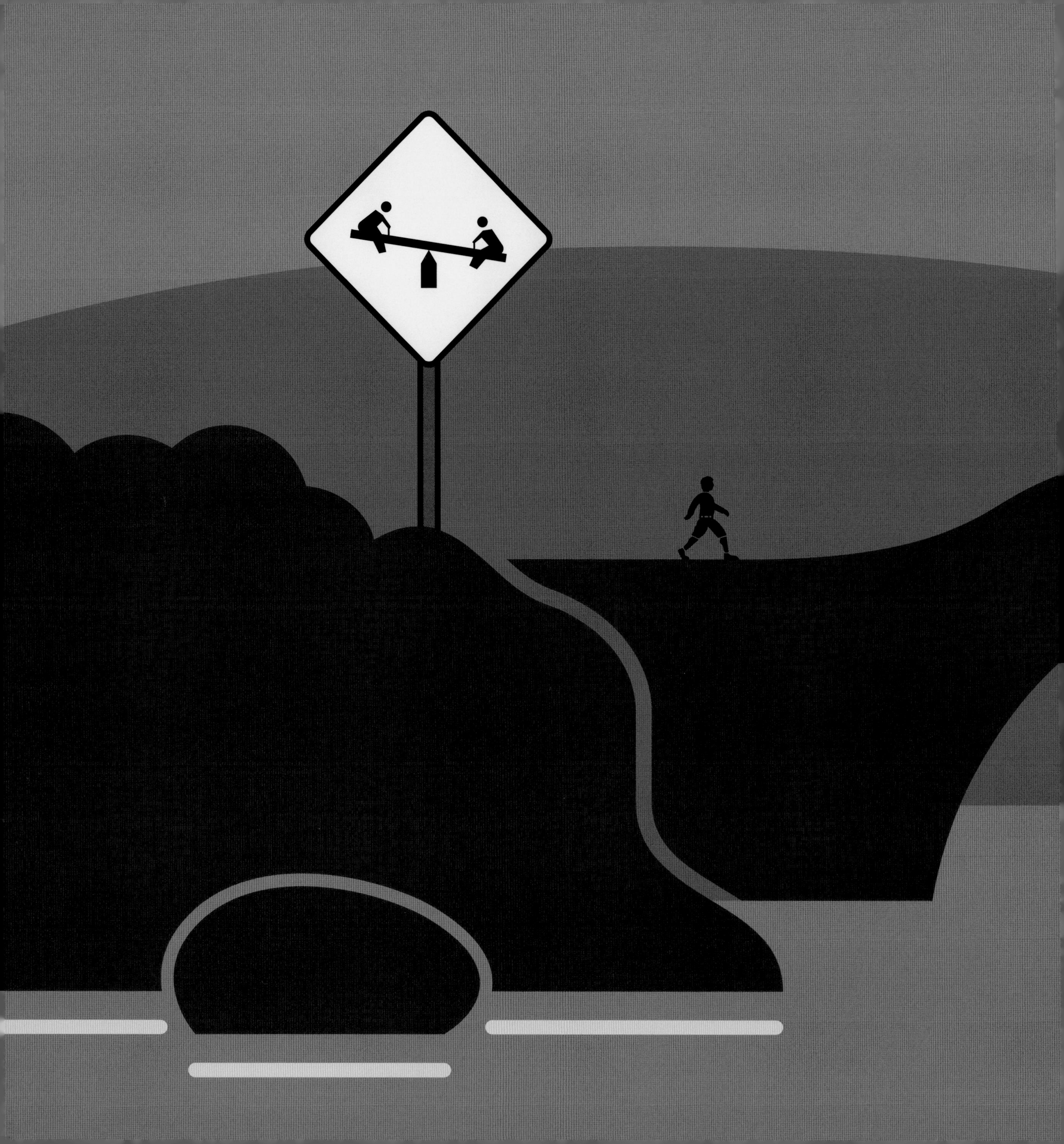

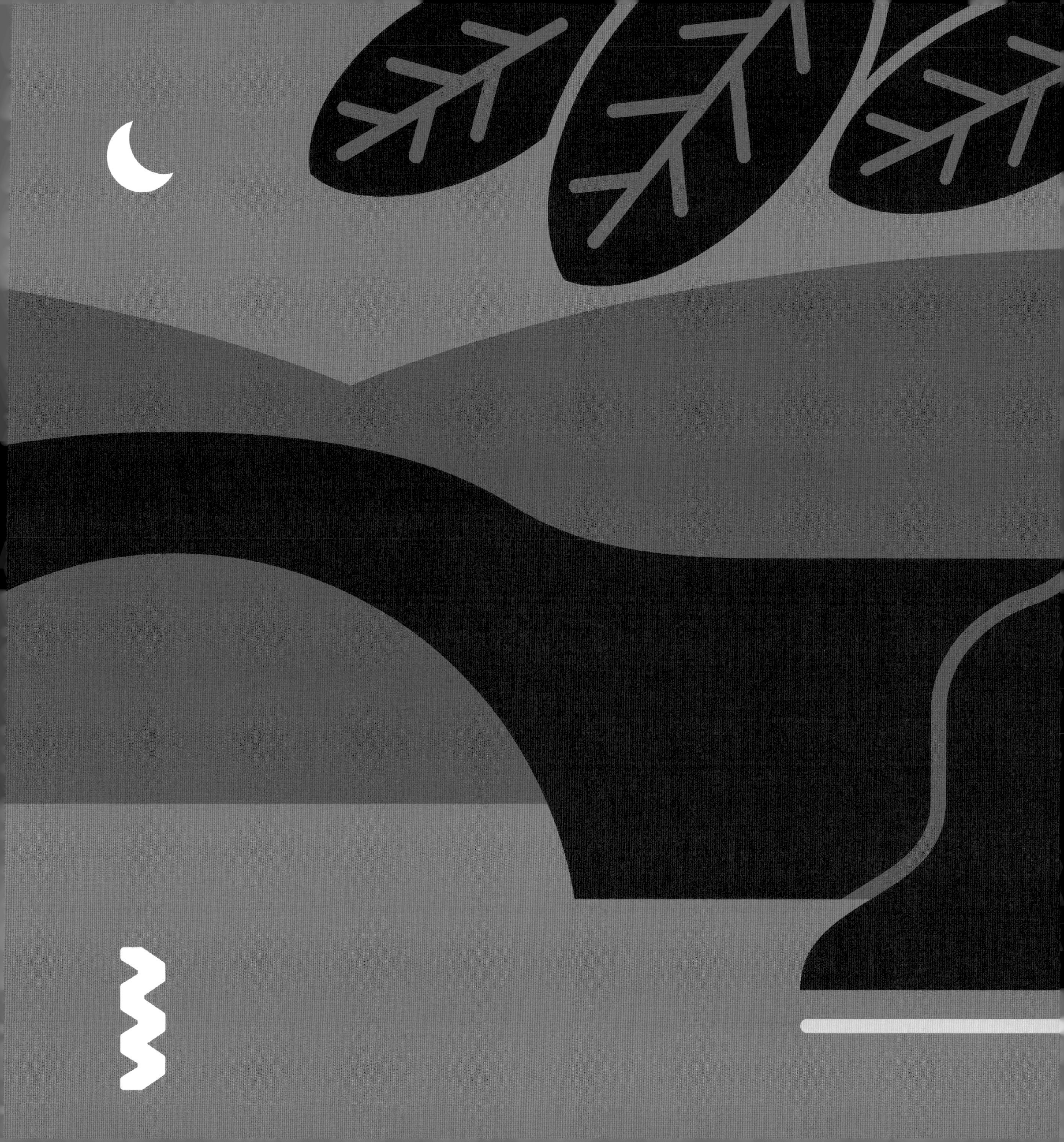

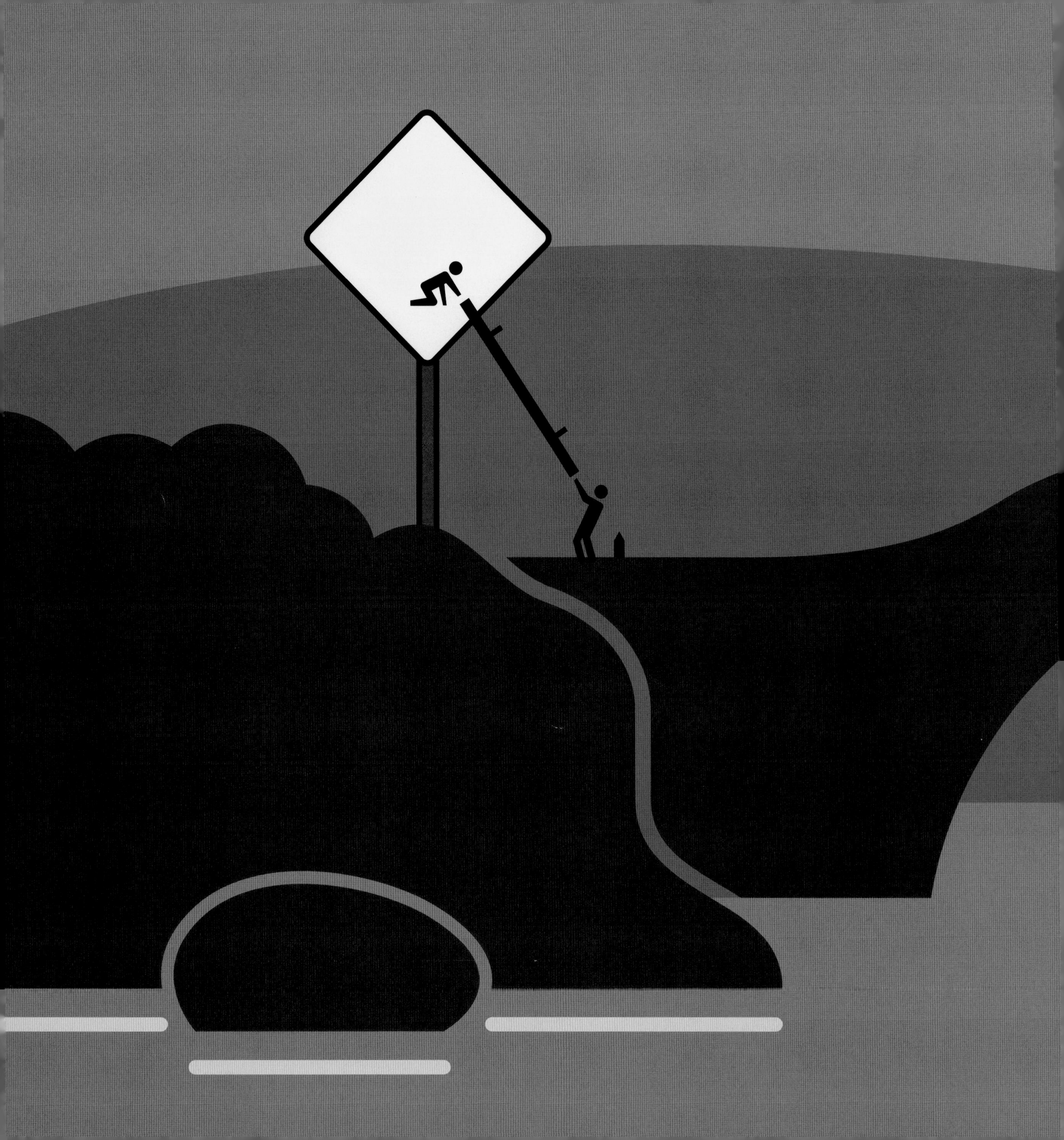

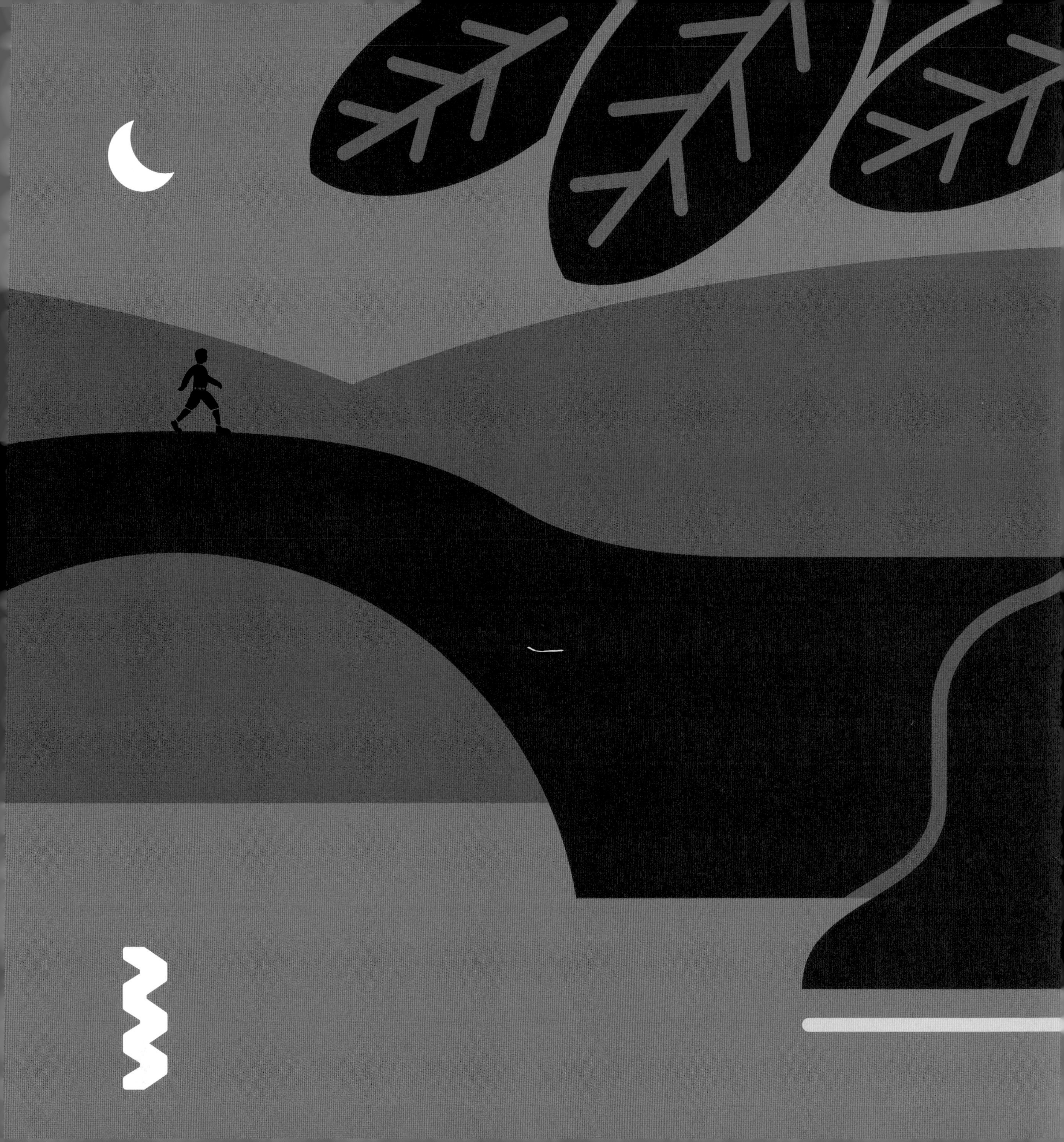

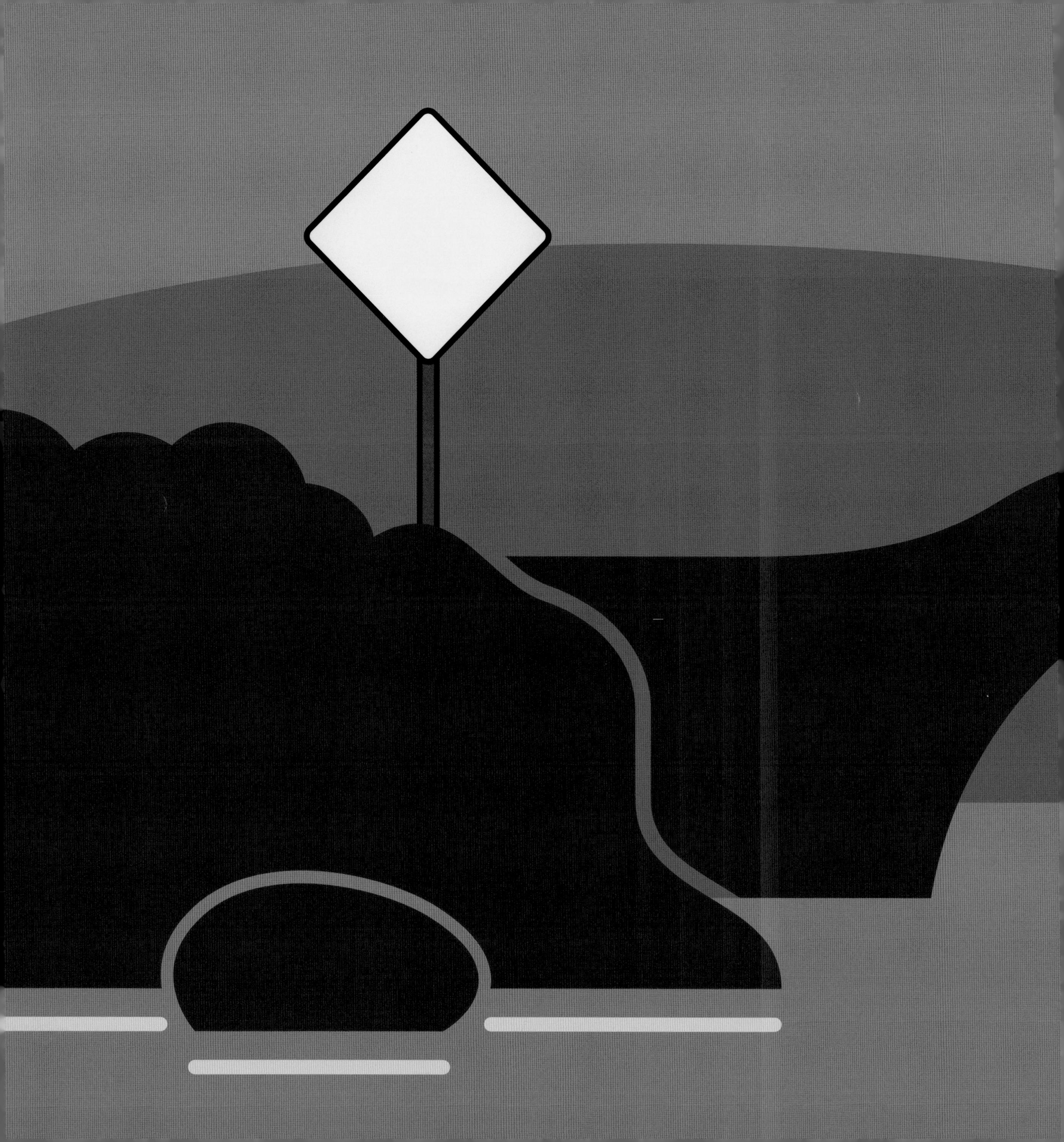

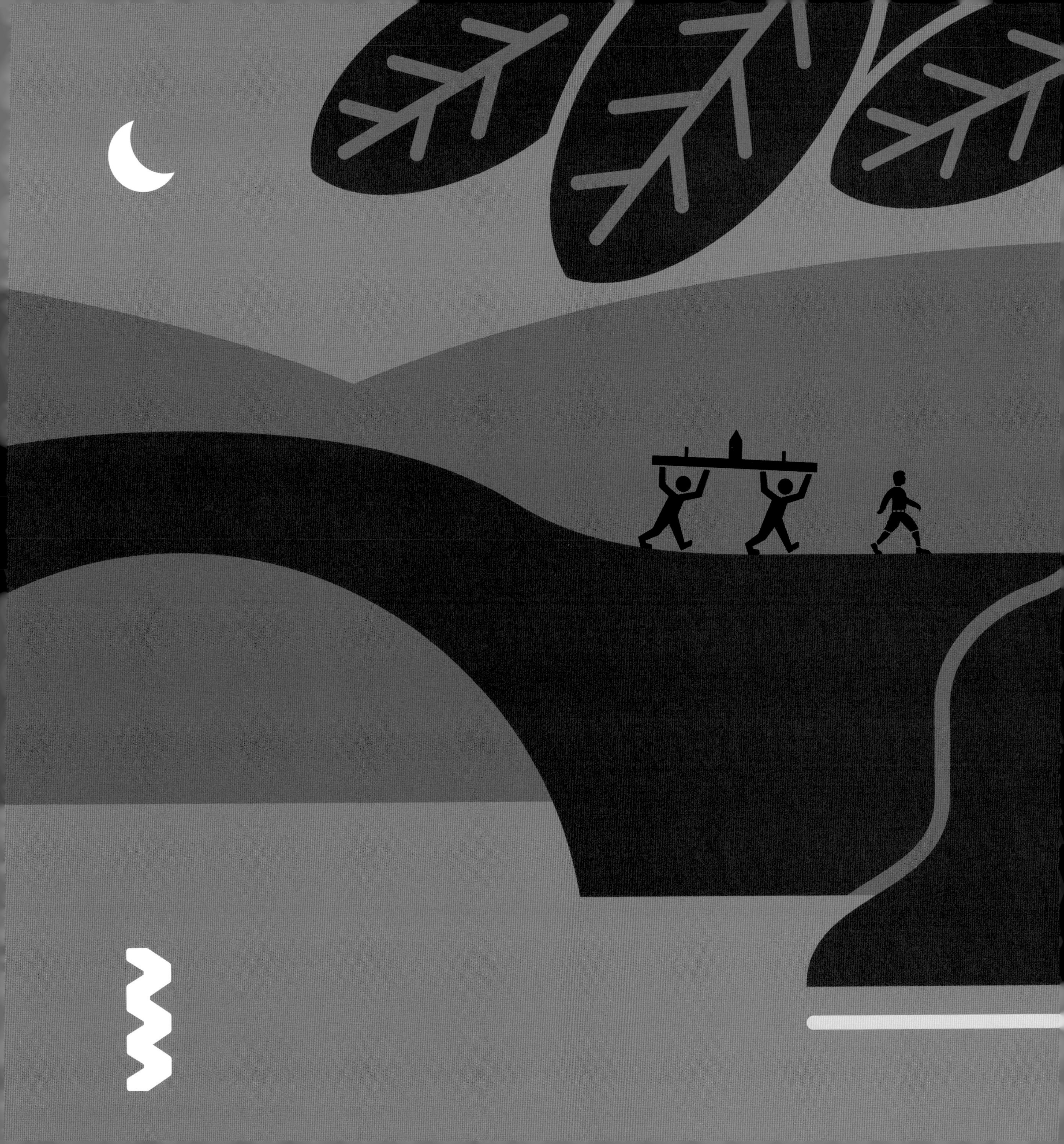

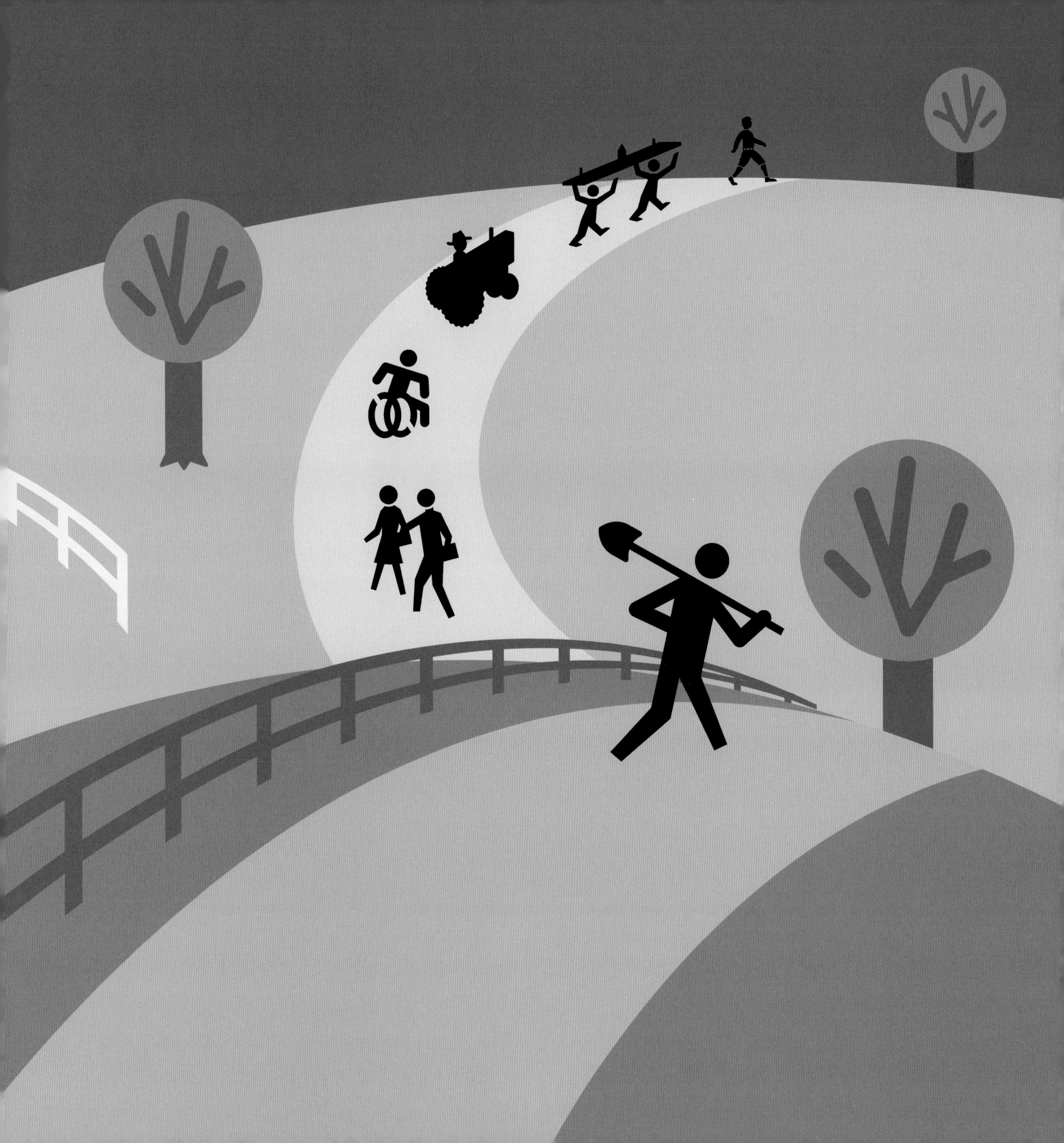

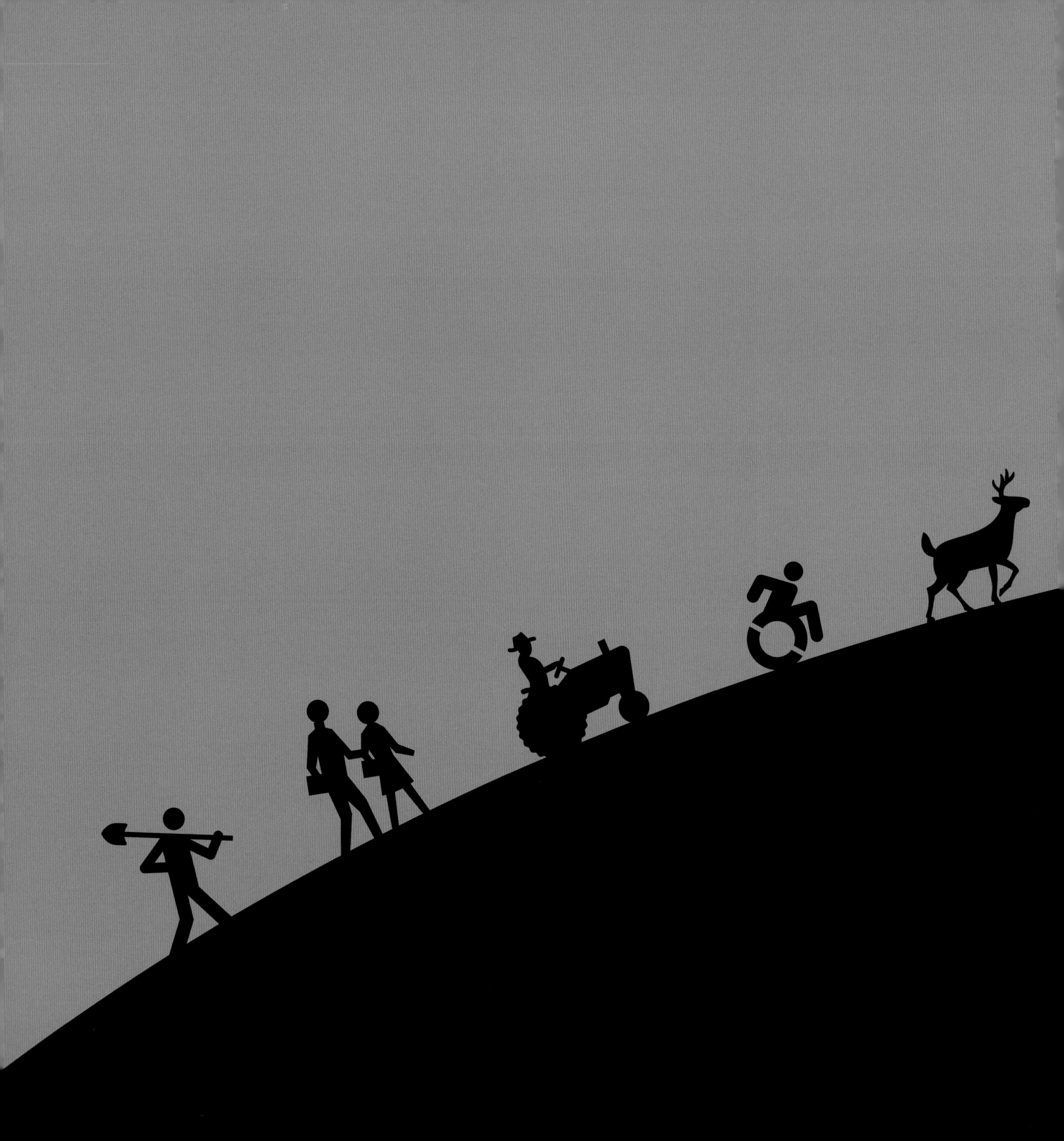

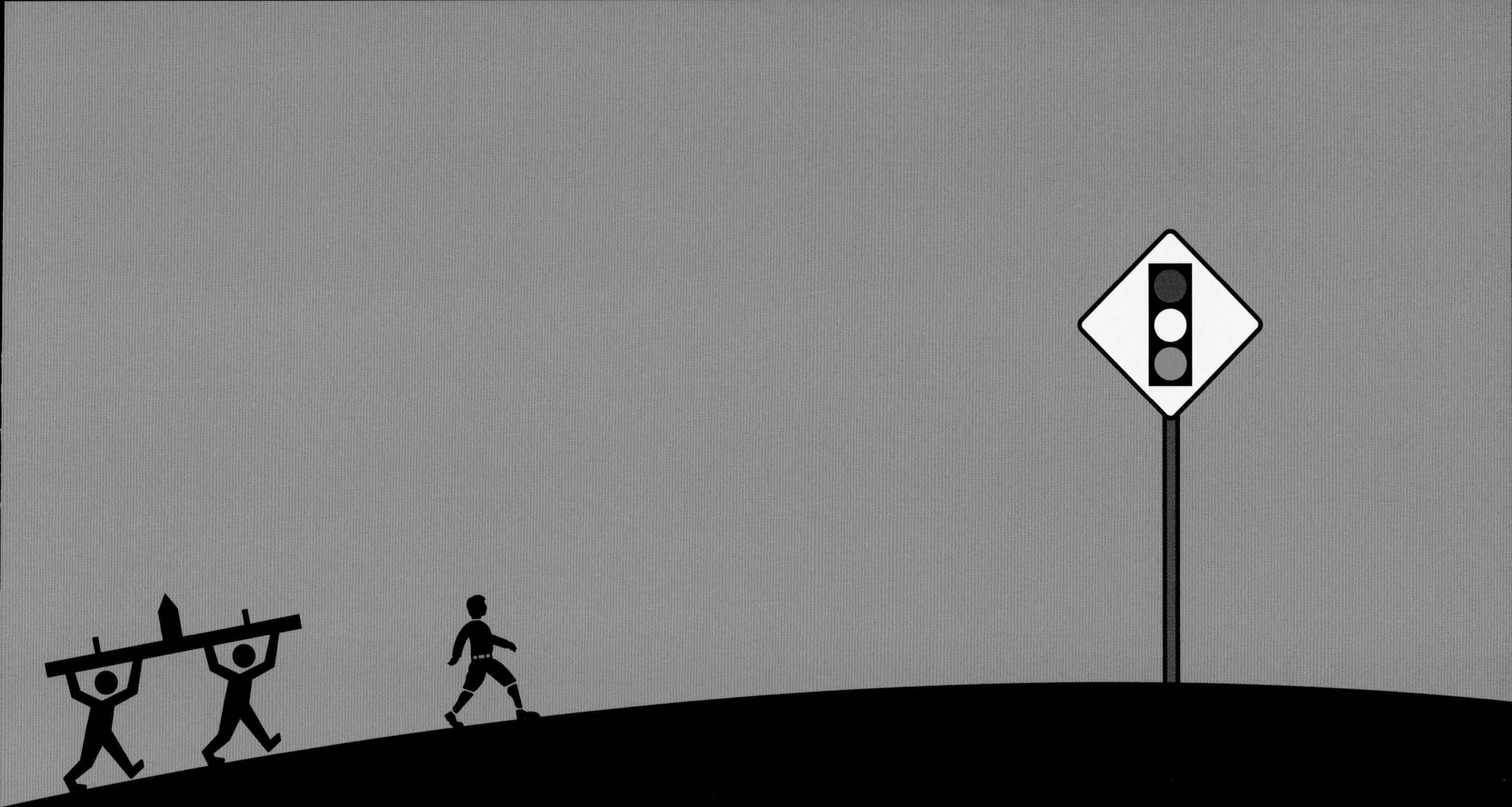

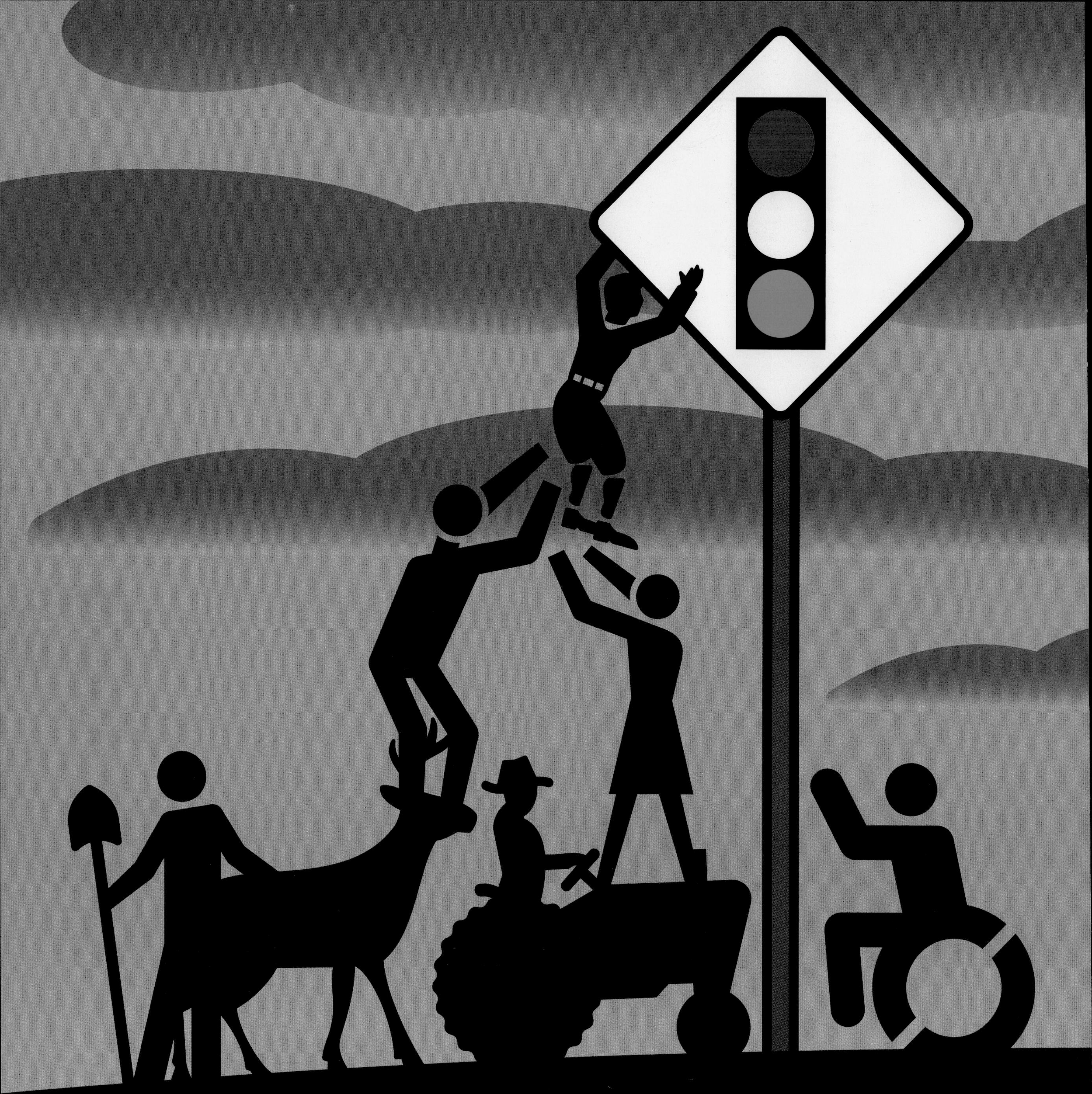

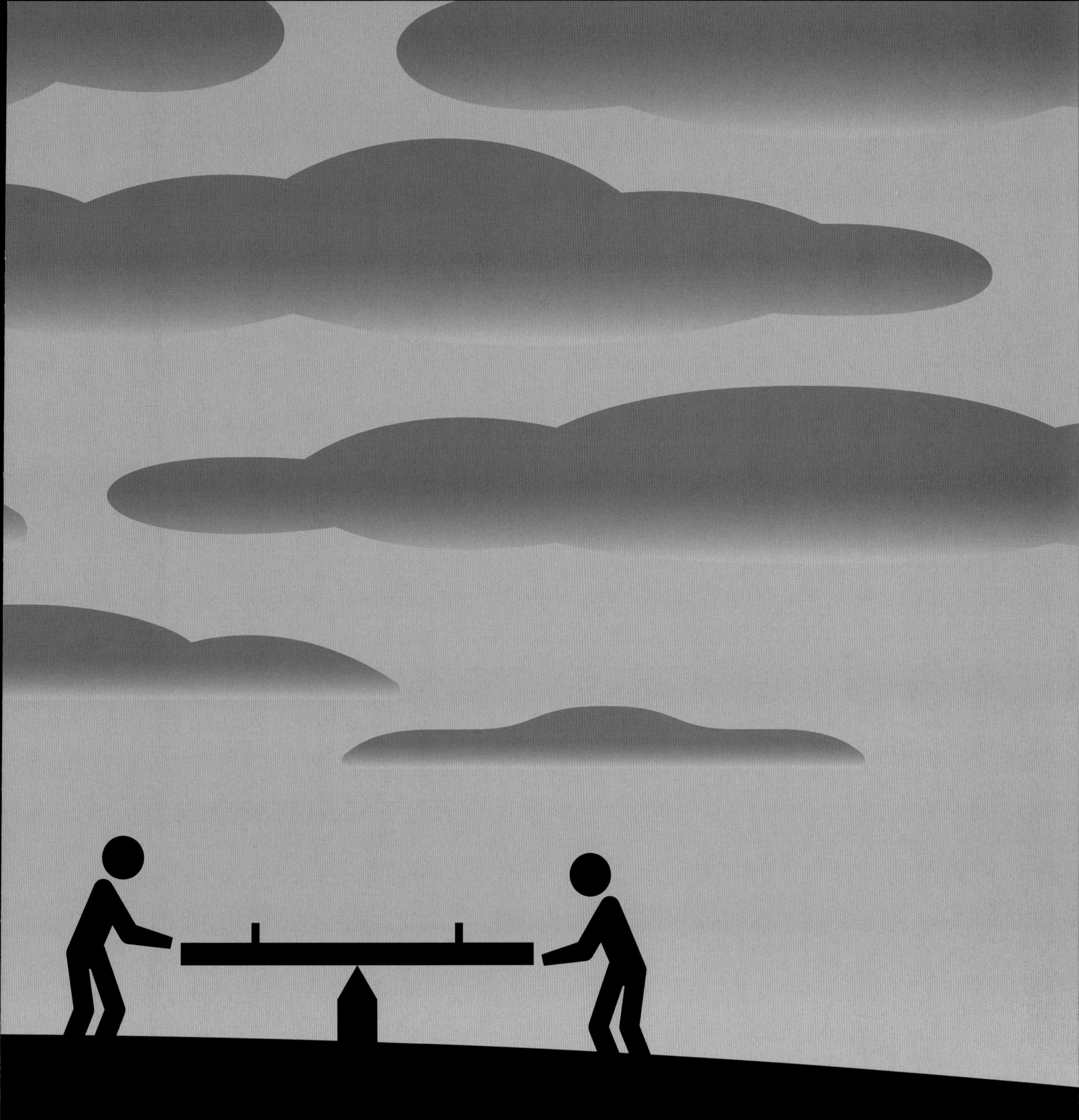

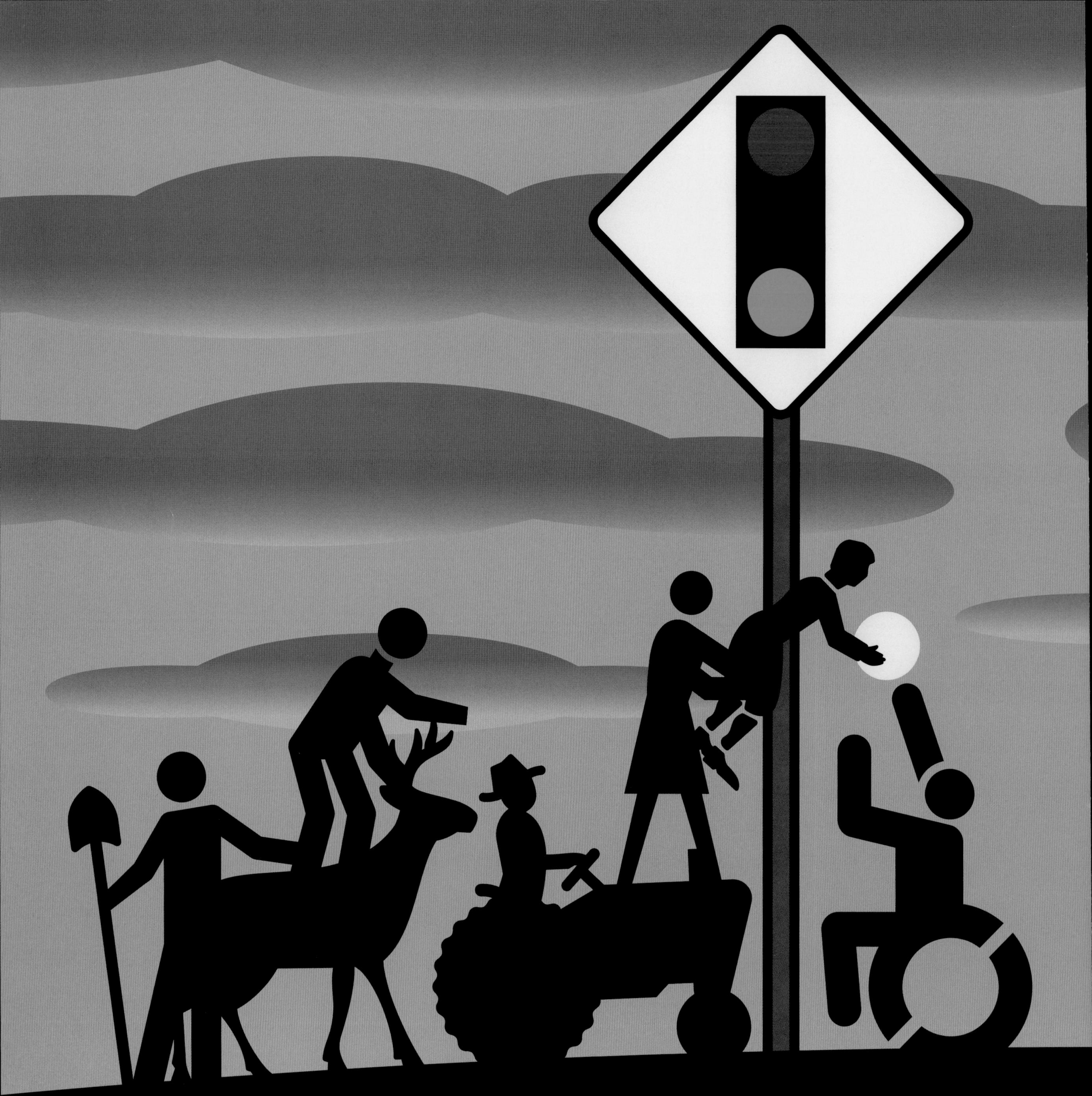

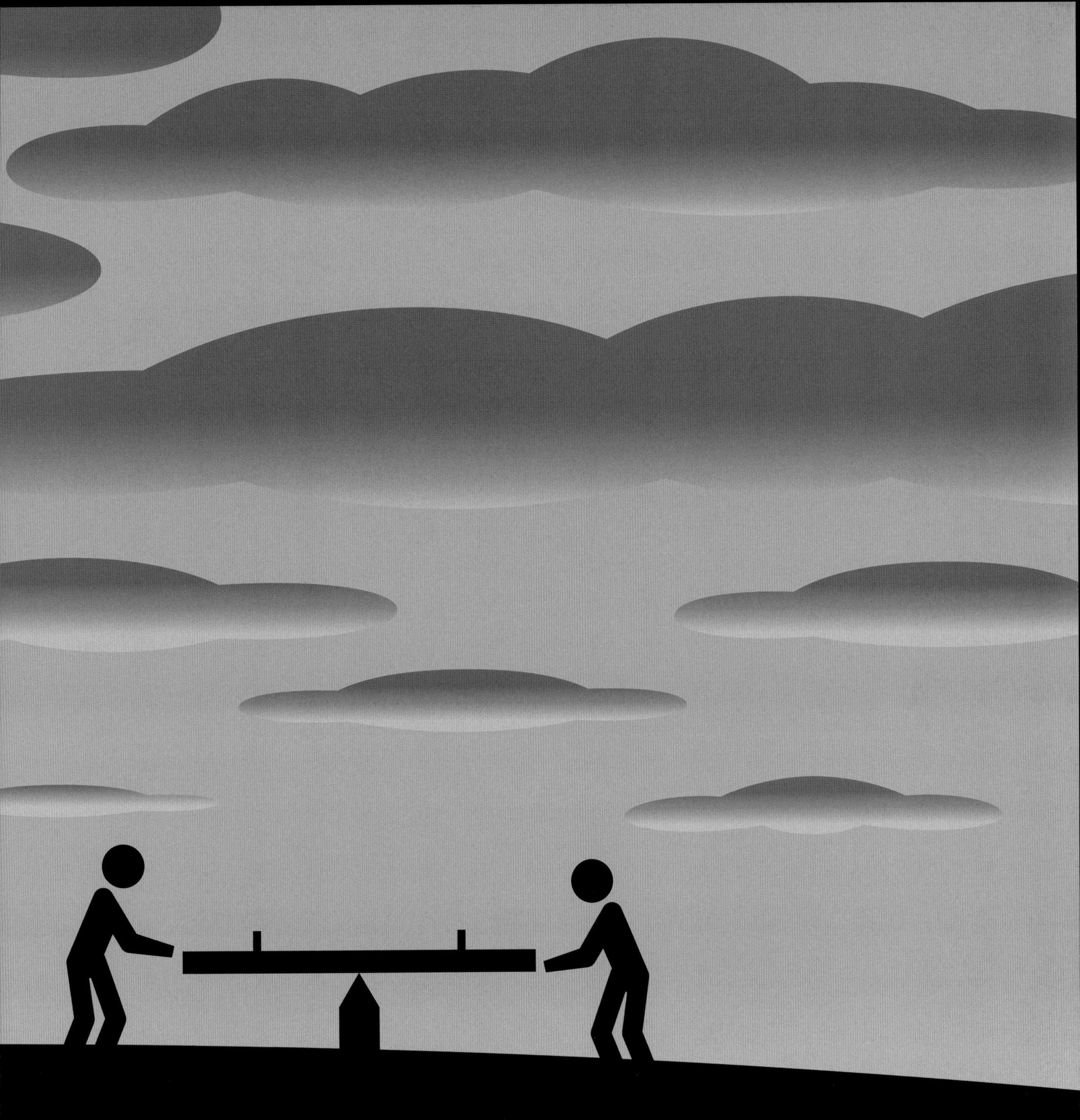

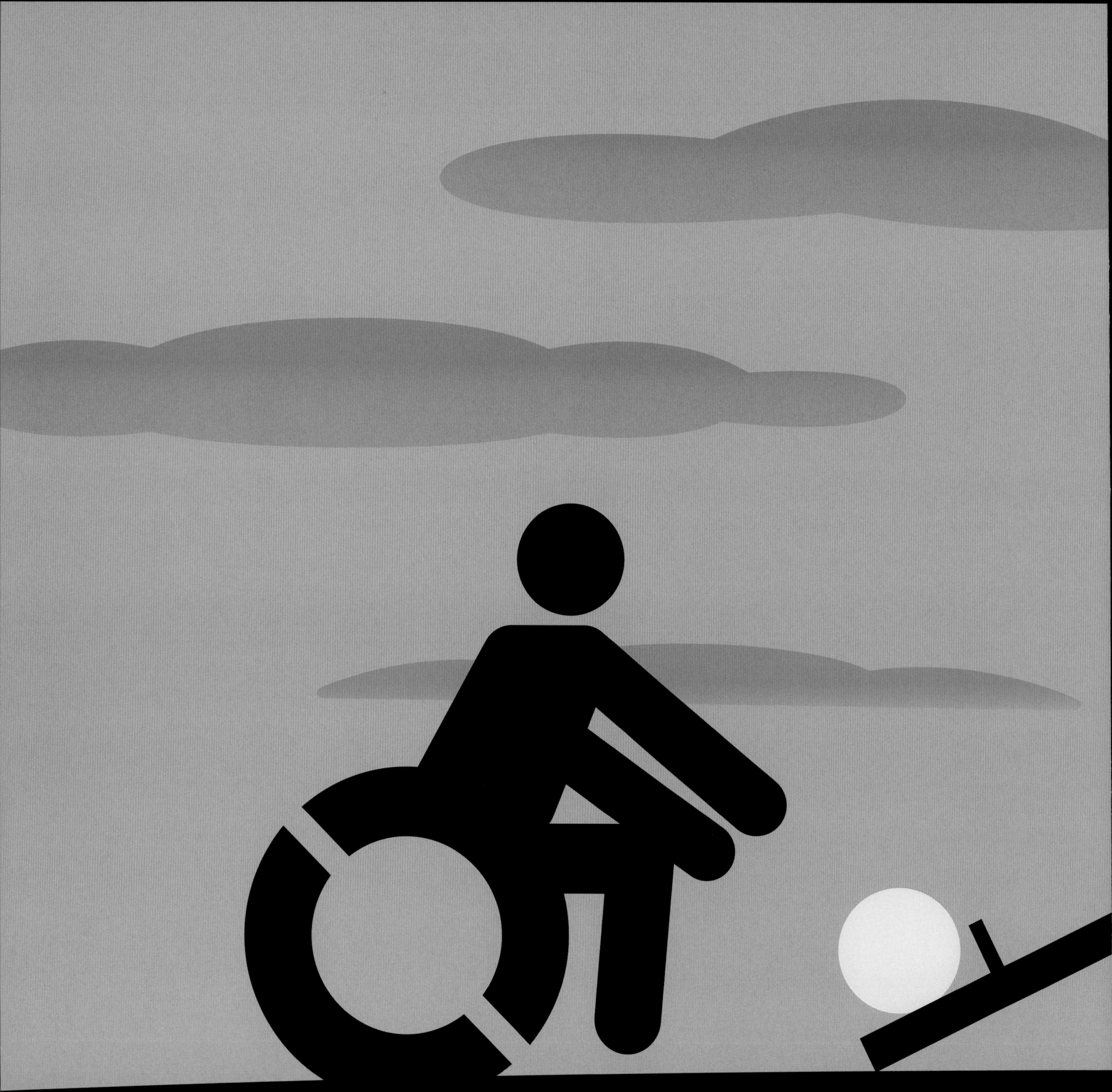

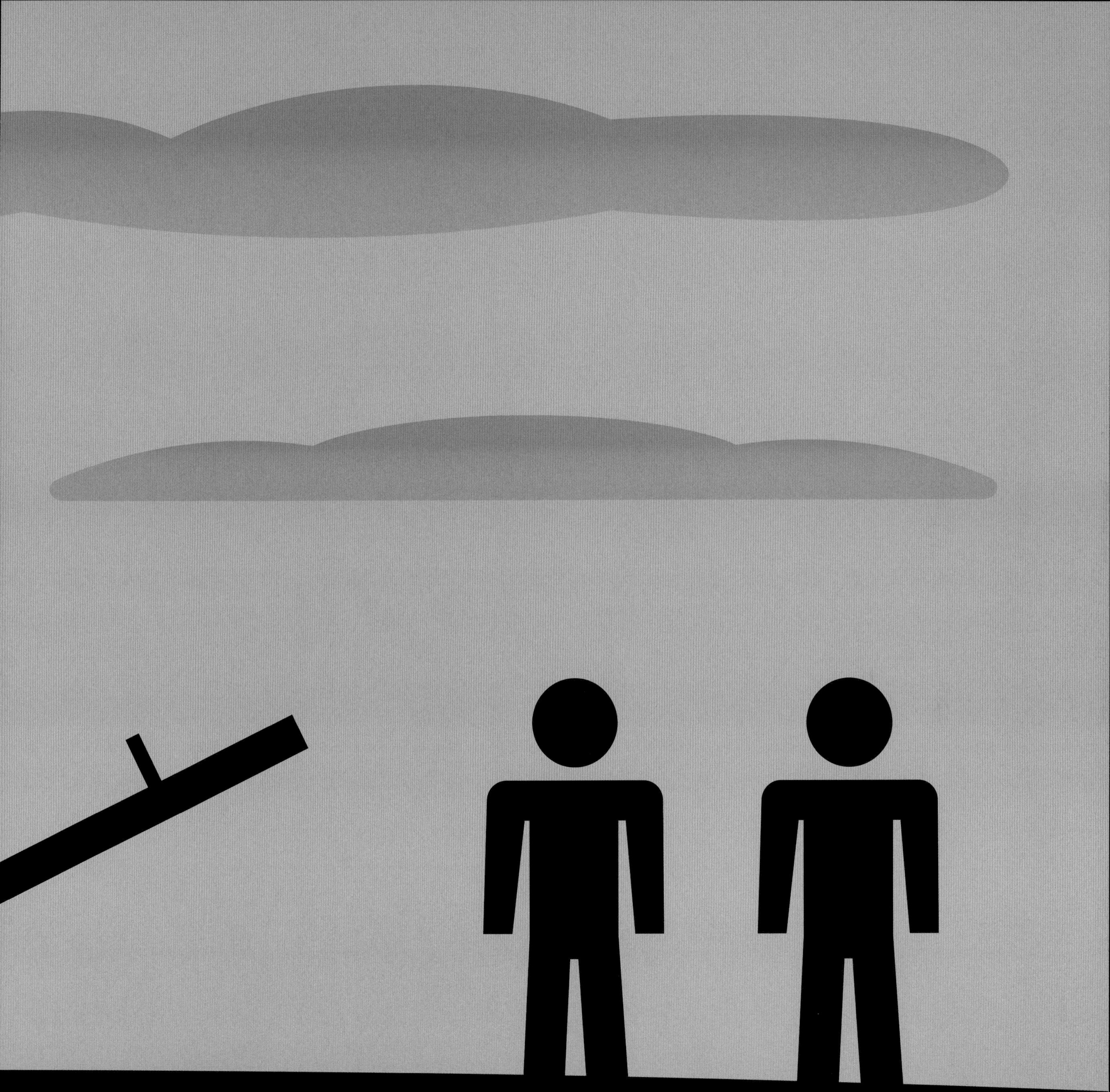

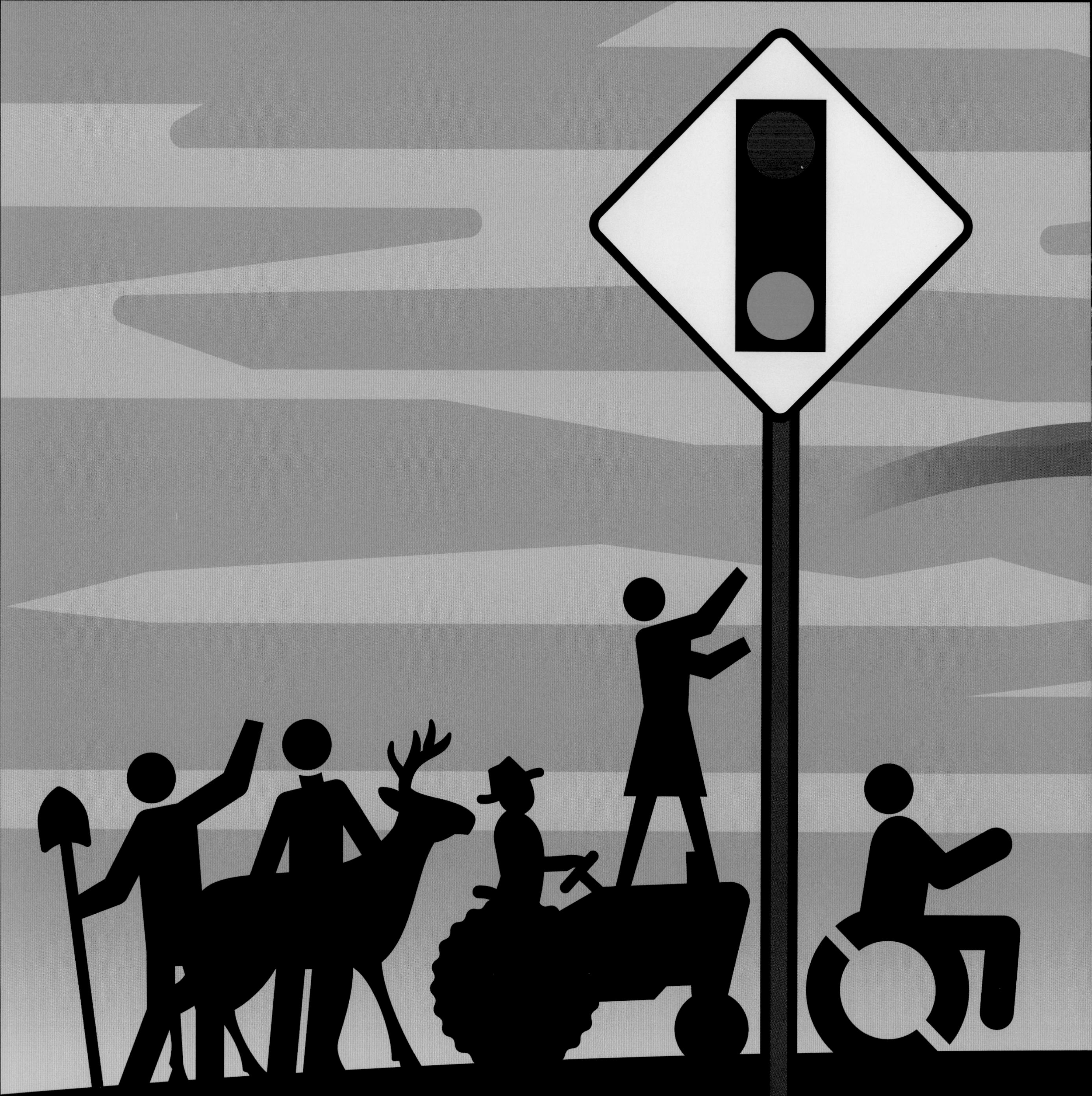

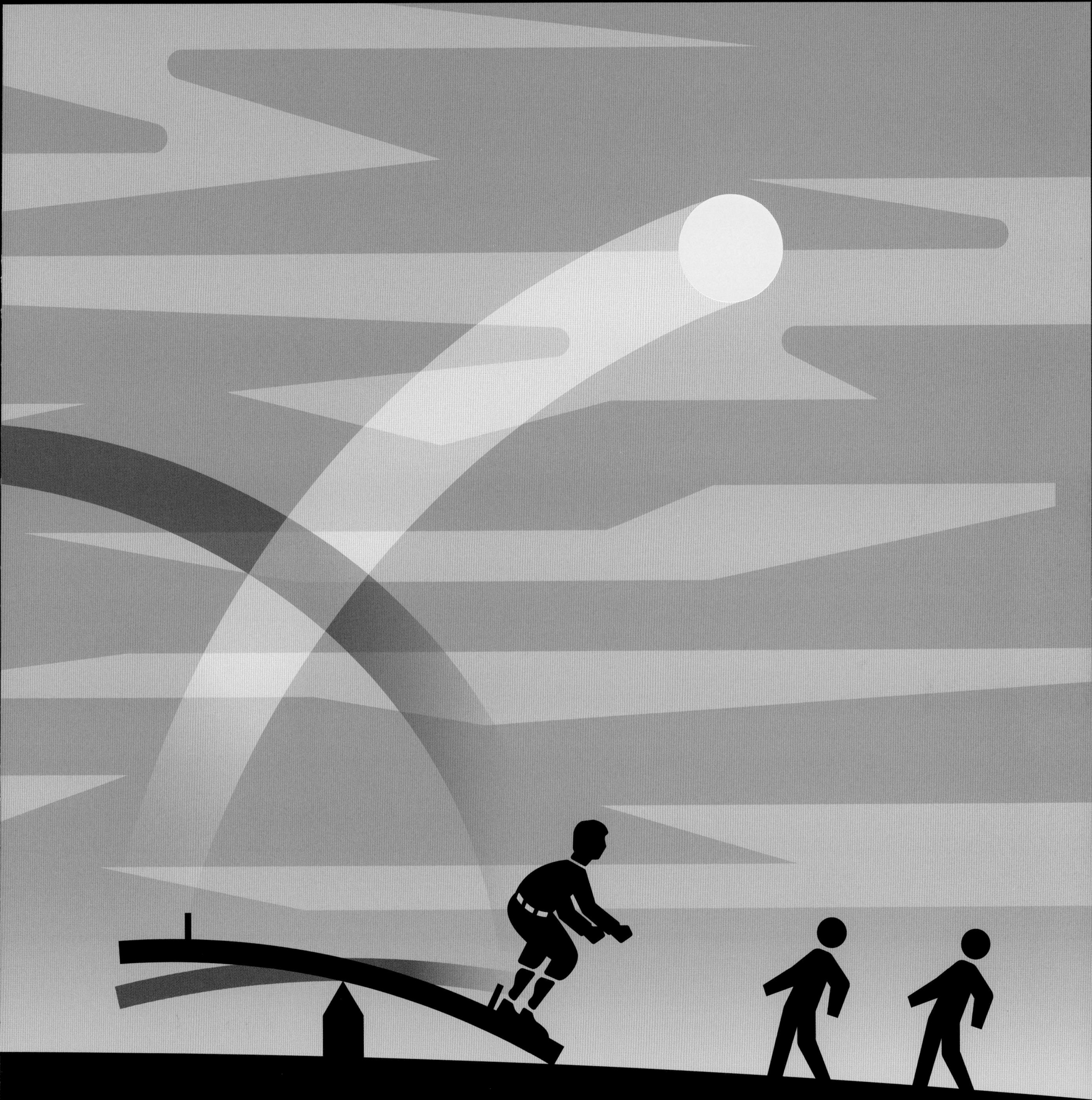

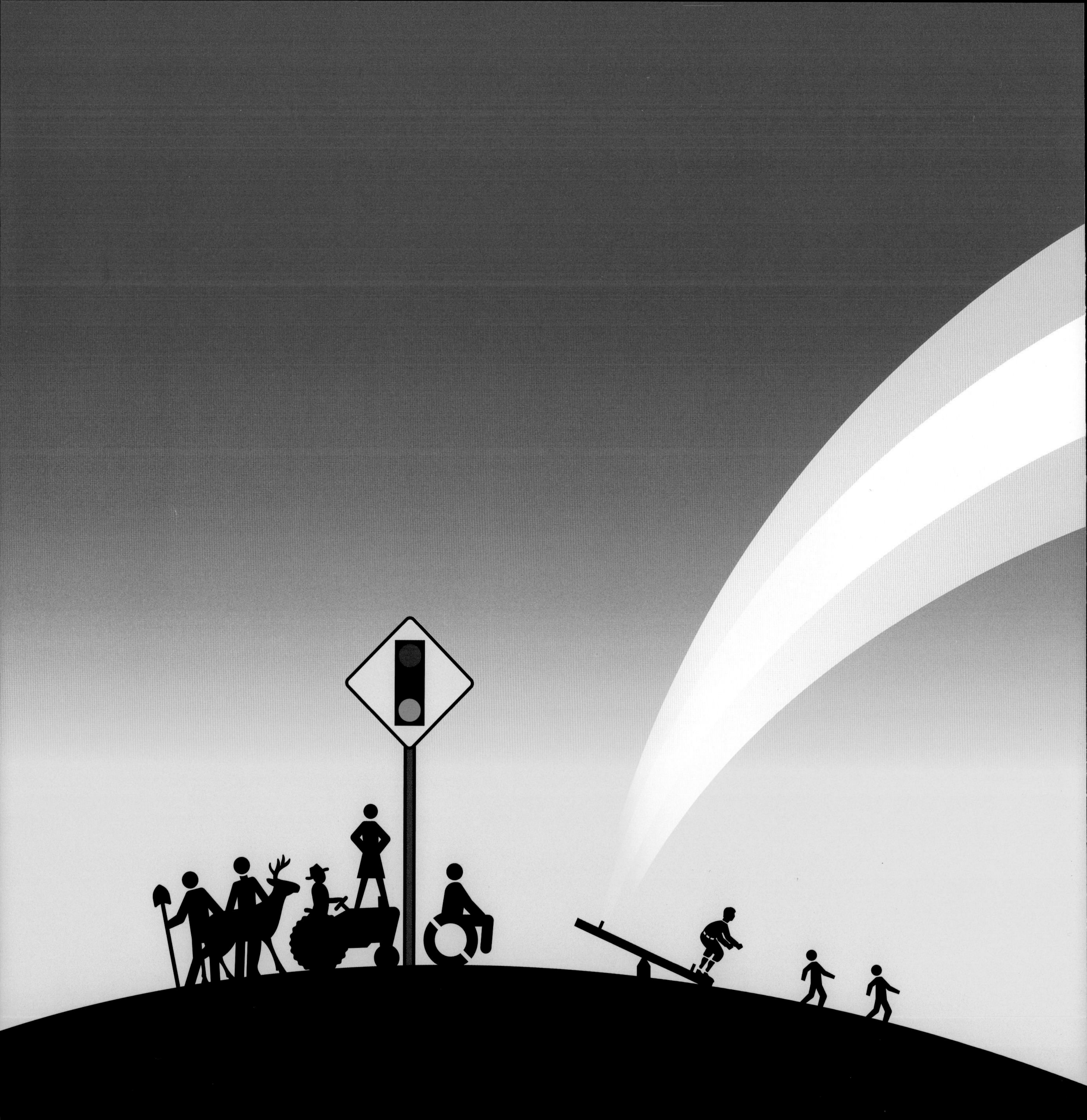

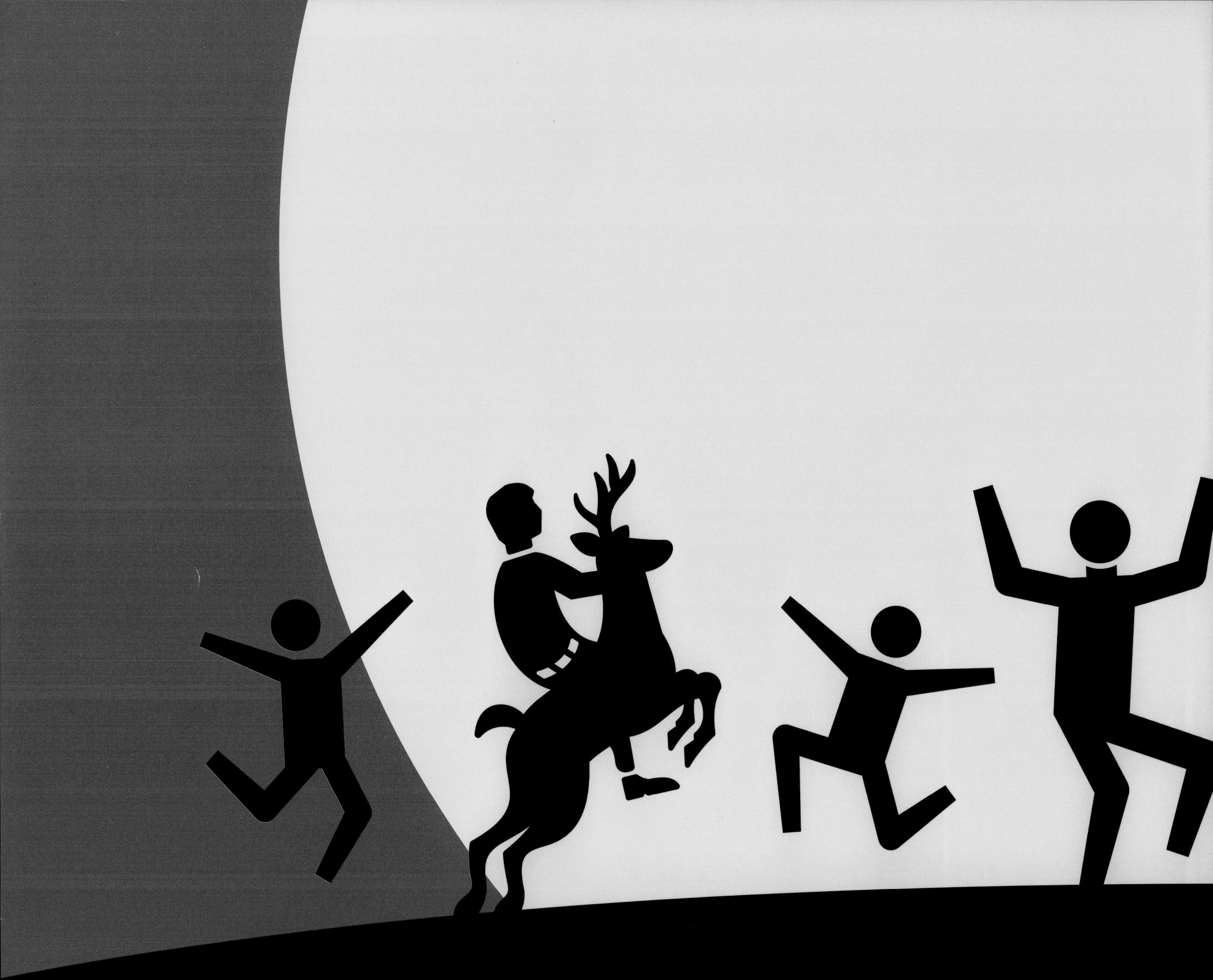

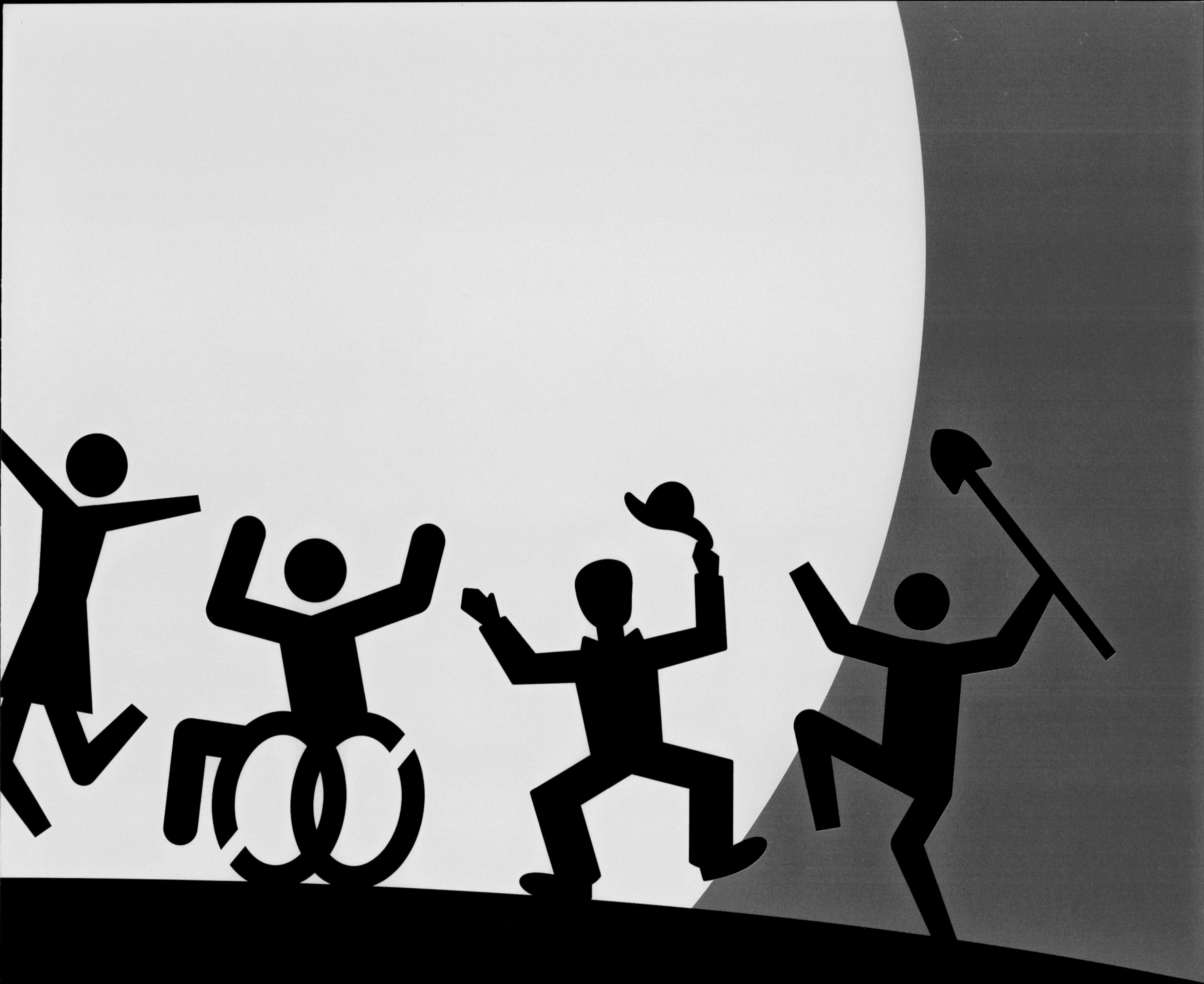

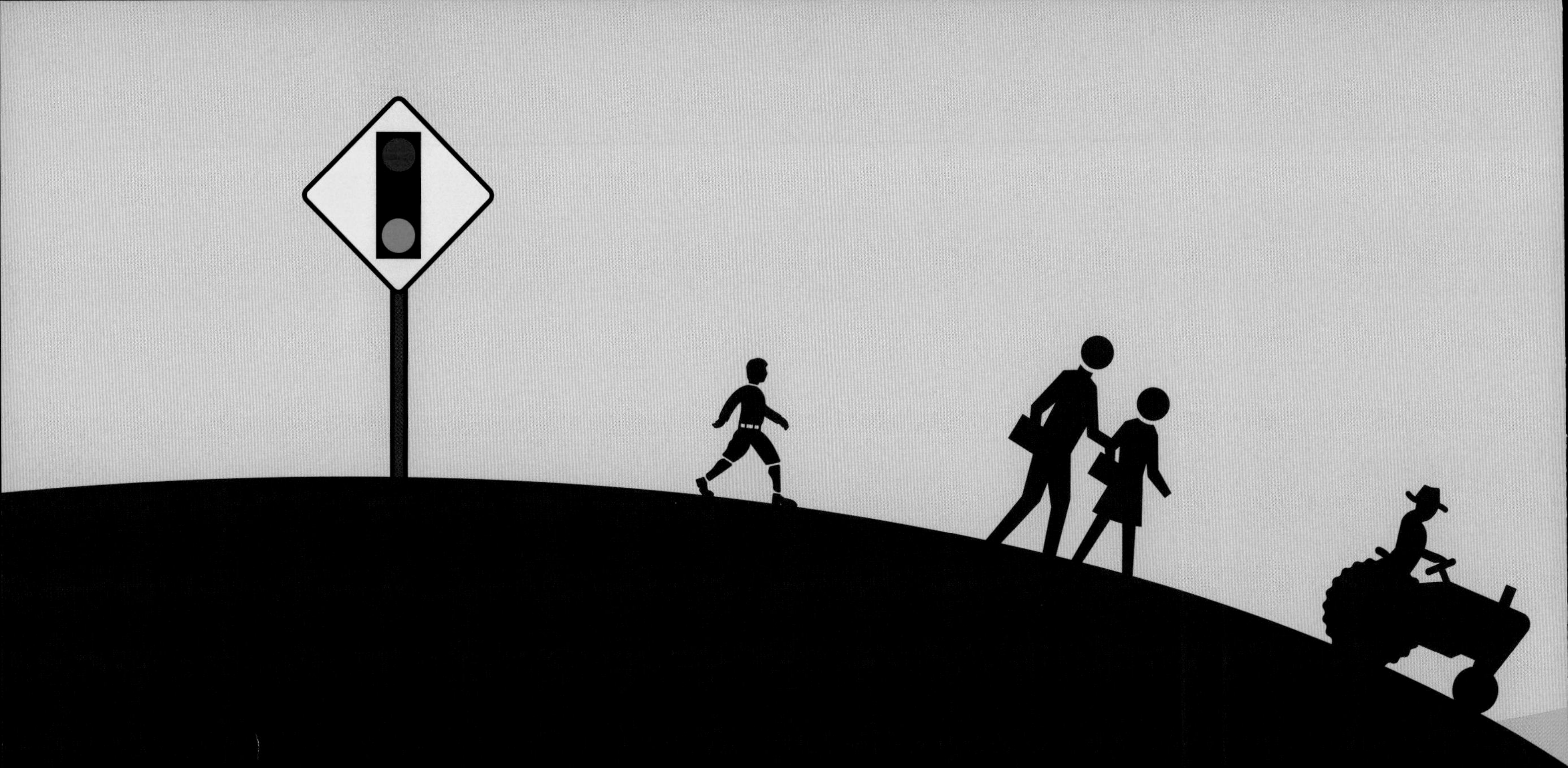

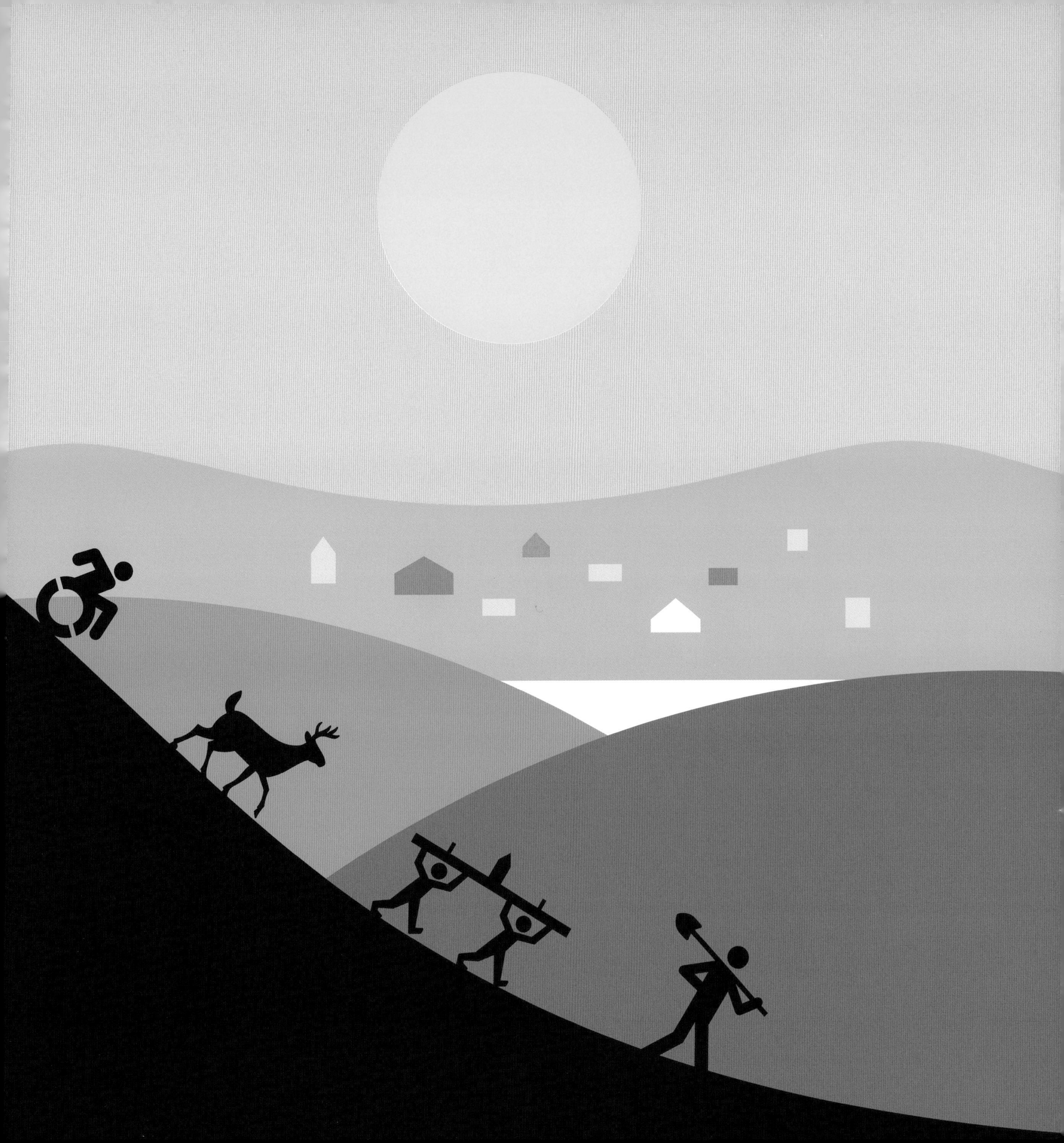